"We Could Get Married."

If Violet had nailed him with a cattle prod, JT couldn't have been more stunned. "Married?"

"In name only, of course." She offered him a cheeky grin. "There's nothing in my uncle's will that prevents me from marrying the shares away."

"Since he knew we'd never get married, it probably never crossed his mind."

She cocked her head and regarded him solemnly. "And how did he know something like that?"

"I told him I had no intention of starting anything up with you. It was an easy promise to make. You really aren't my type."

She stared at him for several seconds. But then her hand stole across his leg, midthigh, and lingered.

"You aren't my type either." But her husky tone and the come-get-me-big-boy look in her eyes said the exact opposite. "So that should make an in-name-only marriage between us a snap."

* * *

A Merger by Marriage is part of the Las Vegas Nights trilogy: Where love is the biggest gamble of all!

* * *

If you're on Twitter,
tell us what you think of Harlequin Desire!
#harlequindesire

Dear Reader,

I know when most people think of Las Vegas, they picture high-energy casinos and spectacular shows that once featured showgirls and now costumed acrobats. For me, it's the history of the town and the people who lived—and died—to make it what it is today.

The idea for my second Las Vegas Nights book came to me after reading several books on Las Vegas history. Back when the mob ran the town, lots of people disappeared. It led me to consider how many people travel to Vegas and how dangerous the issue of identity theft can be.

So I wondered what if my hero's father wasn't who he claimed to be? What if there was no definitive proof that he'd stolen someone's identity?

Trusting those closest to him wasn't something JT Stone developed growing up. Violet Fontaine knows this and is working hard to convince her new husband she only wants what's best for him. But she knows a secret that, if it comes out, may cost her the man she loves.

I hope you enjoy this second installment of Las Vegas Nights. Find more information about my books at my website, www.catschield.net.

All the best!

Cat Schield

A MERGER BY MARRIAGE

—

CAT SCHIELD

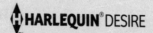

Recycling programs
for this product may
not exist in your area.

ISBN-13: 978-0-373-73317-0

A MERGER BY MARRIAGE

Copyright © 2014 by Catherine Schield

Printed in U.S.A.

Books by Cat Schield

Harlequin Desire

Meddling with a Millionaire #2094
A Win-Win Proposition #2116
Unfinished Business #2153
The Rogue's Fortune #2192
A Tricky Proposition #2214
The Nanny Trap #2253
At Odds with the Heiress #2279
A Merger by Marriage #2304

*Las Vegas Nights

Other titles by this author available in ebook format.

CAT SCHIELD

has been reading and writing romance since high school. Although she graduated from college with a B.A. in business, her idea of a perfect career was writing books for Harlequin. And now, after winning the Romance Writers of America 2010 Golden Heart Award for series contemporary romance, that dream has come true. Cat lives in Minnesota with her daughter, Emily, and their Burmese cat. When she's not writing sexy, romantic stories for Harlequin Desire, she can be found sailing with friends on the St. Croix River, or in more exotic locales like the Caribbean and Europe. She loves to hear from readers. Find her at www.catschield.com. Follow her on Twitter, @catschield.

For Kevan Lyon, my fabulous agent.

One

With his arm stretched across the back of the black leather couch, JT Stone sipped one of Rick's signature cocktails and brooded over a woman.

Tonight Violet Fontaine wore a black, skin-tight mini with long sleeves and a neckline that concealed her delicate collarbones. Despite the snug fit, the dress looked modest when viewed from the front. But the back of the dress. Oh, the back. A wide V bared an expanse of golden skin, criss-crossed by spaghetti thin straps from her nape to the indent of her waist. As he suspected the design intended, his gaze was drawn to the curve of her tight, round backside.

His fingers twitched as he imagined holding those luscious curves in his hands. Before he'd met Violet six years ago he'd been a diehard breast and thigh man. These days he was on a mission to find a butt better than hers. To date he hadn't found one. Good thing she had no idea what she did to him or he might lose something more irreplaceable than his favorite bartender.

The resident mixologist of Fontaine Chic's lobby bar Baccarat, Rick was a genius when it came to creating unique cocktails. Tonight JT was having Rick's version of a dirty martini in the lounge. His excuse for showing up six nights a week was that he was wooing Rick back to Titanium where he belonged.

JT finished the last of his drink. Who was he kidding? In the year since Rick had switched employers, JT was here most nights because Violet swung through on her rounds at exactly eleven-fifteen and lingered to chat with the clientele. As the proprietor of the Fontaine Chic, she was very hands-on.

"Another drink, JT?" The waitress cocked her head and smiled warmly at him.

"Sure." Why not? He nodded toward Violet. "And whatever she's drinking."

Charlene followed his gaze. "You know she doesn't drink when she's working."

"Maybe tonight she'll make an exception for me."

"Maybe." But Charlene's tone said something completely different.

"Would you send her over?"

The nightly ritual made the waitress's lips curve in wry humor. "Sure."

Violet herself brought his drink over, setting it before him with practiced ease. "Rick said this is what you're drinking tonight."

"Will you join me?"

When she shook her head, the diamond drops dangling from her earlobes swayed seductively. "I'm working."

"And I'm your best customer."

"You're a fan of Rick's, not Fontaine Chic."

"I'm a fan of you," he murmured and her eyes widened briefly as if startled by his admission. Was it possible she was oblivious to his interest? Not one of the waitresses thought he came here every night just to drink.

It did no good to remind himself that he liked his women

curvy, blonde and agreeable. That with her long lean frame inherited from her showgirl mother and her father's wavy brown hair, she was not his type. Or that her strong-willed personality had been cultivated by his estranged uncle, Tiberius Stone, her surrogate father. A man who blamed JT's father for orchestrating his disinheritance.

"You can take a couple minutes," he said, gesturing to the empty space beside him.

Her eyebrow arched at his implied command, but she settled sideways on the couch and crossed her long legs. She'd fastened her waist-length hair into a high, sleek ponytail. The look was both modern and retro and showed off her large brown eyes and bold cheekbones to great advantage.

With the toe of her black stiletto a mere inch from his pant leg, she propped her elbow on the back of the couch, rested her cheek on her palm and waited for him to speak. Quick to smile, she was the most upbeat, optimistic person he'd ever met. She was sunlight to his shadow. Forever close, always untouchable.

He sipped his drink and surveyed her over the rim. The dark circles beneath her eyes told him she was working harder than ever since Tiberius had been murdered several weeks ago.

"You should take some time off," he said, aware that what she did was none of his business.

"And do what? Sit around and grieve?" She must have heard the edge in her tone because after a long sigh, she continued on a milder note. "I know it's what most people do when they lose a parent, but I can't think of a better way to honor Tiberius's memory than to work."

JT nodded in understanding. "I'm sure he'd approve."

Although he'd been given the middle name, Tiberius, after his mother's younger brother, until the last few months JT had never had the chance to know his uncle by anything other than reputation. JT had been raised in Miami where Stone Properties had their headquarters. Tiberius rarely left Vegas. And the bad blood between Tiberius and his brother-in-law and JT's father, Preston Rhodes, made any chance of a relationship between JT and his uncle impossible.

The hard feelings between Tiberius and Preston went back twenty-five years. According to what JT had gleaned from family friends, Preston had accused Tiberius of embezzling from Stone Properties and had convinced James Stone to fire his son. Then, five years later, James had died and JT's father had used his influence over his wife, Fiona Stone—bowing to pressure from her father, she'd never taken her husband's last name—to get the board of directors to vote in favor of making him chairman and CEO.

"Thanks for coming to the memorial service this morning," Violet said. "I know you and Tiberius weren't close, but lately he'd talked a lot about how he regretted all the years he kept you out of his life and how he wished he'd gotten to know you."

Regret tightened in his chest. "I had no idea Tiberius felt that way." JT sucked in a deep breath and let it out slowly.

When he'd arrived in Las Vegas to run the local family operations, his opinion of his uncle had been formed by what he knew about Tiberius from his father and grandfather. Although relations between him and his uncle stayed tense for many years, after seeing how much Violet admired Tiberius, plus all the positive things said about his uncle by other Las Vegas businessmen, JT had begun to suspect that if Tiberius had done what his father had accused him of, there'd been a good reason.

"When it came to your family, he could be hard-headed," Violet said with a faint smile. "And he really hated your dad."

"The feeling was definitely mutual."

Violet remained lost in thought for a moment. "Lately he'd mentioned quite a few times that he thought you'd do a terrific job running Stone Properties."

The compliment landed a direct hit in his gut. He wished he'd had a chance to get to know his uncle the way Violet did. Now it was too late. "I'm leaving the company."

JT heard himself say the words and wondered at his impromptu disclosure. He hadn't divulged his inner thoughts to anyone. Not even his cousin, Brent, and they were as close as brothers. JT peered into his drink. Had Rick infused some sort of truth serum into the cocktail? JT set the glass down. When he looked up, he caught Violet staring at him in surprise.

"Why would you do that?"

"When I turned thirty two months ago, I gained control of my trust fund and the thirty percent of Stone Properties shares my mother left to me when she died. This enabled me to dig into the finances and see what my father has been doing lately."

"And?"

"The properties are overleveraged. My father's been borrowing too much trying to expand and with each property that gets built, our resources are stretched closer to their breaking point." In his gut was a ball of frustration that had been growing steadily these last sixty days.

"I had no idea." Sympathy made her voice soft. She felt sorry for him and he hated it. "Have you shared your concerns with your father?"

It wasn't like him to disclose his difficulties to anyone, least of all someone as tightly connected to the competition as Violet. But then, she wasn't just anyone. She was special. Through her he was linked to a part of his family he'd never known and just being around her made him feel less alone.

JT picked up his drink once more. "He won't listen and

since he controls the majority of the shares, I don't have leverage to affect current policy."

"If you leave Stone Properties, what are you planning to do?"

He'd never been one to show his cards, but Violet's attentiveness made her easy to confide in. She acted as if she had all the time in the world to listen to what ailed him and offer sensible feedback. He'd be a fool not to listen to her opinion as a businesswoman. But it was her friendship he craved. And if he was honest with himself, her body he longed to devour.

"I've been cultivating some investors," he said. "I'm going out on my own. My uncle didn't need the family business to be successful and neither do I."

"Are you sure that's the best idea? Tiberius let your father drive him out of the business and never stopped regretting it."

"No one drove him out," JT corrected her. "Tiberius was caught stealing from the company and was fired."

Her disappointment in him was like clouds passing in front of the sun. "He was framed." She truly believed that. "By your father."

JT sat perfectly still beneath the weight of her accusation while his thought raced. A normal person would rush to defend their father against such slander, but JT had seen the company's financials for himself and knew his father was not telling the stockholders everything. That made him a liar in JT's books. Nor would he ever champion his father after the way Preston had treated JT's mother.

But he wasn't ready to jump on the bash-Preston bandwagon either. As conflicted as JT was about his father, he put a high value on loyalty.

"If that's true," he said, his tone neutral, "all the more reason to break with the company and my father."

Determination flared in her eyes. "Or you could stay and fight for what's yours."

While JT appreciated her spirited defense of his inheritance, he'd been contemplating the wisdom of staying with Stone Properties for a couple years. It was worse now that he had seen the company's financials.

"I hate being powerless to stop him from taking apart all that my grandfather built."

"I can understand that." Without warning her gaze sharpened. "These plans of yours, do they mean you're leaving Las Vegas?"

Was she hoping he wouldn't? The thought of not seeing her every day made him grim. Did it bother her as well?

JT searched her eyes for answers, but saw only curiosity. With Violet, what you saw was what you got. Her openness fascinated him. She never seemed to worry about guarding herself against hurt or disappointment.

It was a major factor in why he'd never pursued her.

Not long after he'd arrived in Las Vegas, he'd run into his uncle and Violet at a charity event. Despite his instant attraction to the twenty-three-year-old, he knew better than to act on his interest. The bad blood between her adopted father and his biological one was a significant barrier. So was JT's playboy lifestyle.

Before he'd moved to Las Vegas, JT had made quite a name for himself in Miami's social scene. Going at life at a reckless pace whether it was fast boats, expensive cars or unavailable women, he hadn't cared whom he hurt as long as he displeased his father.

He liked Violet too much to subject her to his unhealthy family dynamic. Besides, she wasn't a good choice for him. Unlike the women he usually pursued, she would expect things from him. Things he couldn't give her. Openness. Joy. Trust. In order to be with her he'd have to surrender the defenses that muffled his emotions and protected him from pain and disillusionment. She'd lure him out of his comfortable dark cave and require him to find happiness.

How was he supposed to do that when his childhood hadn't given him the tools?

His father believed anything that got in the way of business was bad. As a kid, JT had had that philosophy hammered into his head. His mother had been weakened by her hunger for love. Being ignored by the domineering husband she adored had made her life hell, and she'd started retreating into drugs and alcohol around the time that Tiberius left town. By the time he turned twelve, JT was used to being ignored by his parents, forgotten by his grandfather and alienated from his uncle. Nor was there any family on his father's side. The only person who'd showed any interest in him was his grandmother and she split her time between Miami, Virginia and Kentucky.

Traditional family. Love. JT had never grown up with these things.

Being around Violet gave him a glimpse of what a normal personal life could be. The love she had for her sisters, her mother and Tiberius made him long to be included in her circle. But he couldn't take the steps needed to put himself there. Nor could he leave well enough alone either. The need to connect remained. A tantalizing temptation. One of his deep, dark secrets.

So he visited Fontaine Chic night after night and sat in the bar. He craved a relationship with Violet, but had no idea how to go about having one. In casino terms, he was betting the minimum. He'd never win big, but he wasn't going to lose everything either. Playing without risk was not how he lived. He got a rush from flinging his body into danger, but gambling with his heart was something else entirely.

"I don't know what the future holds," he responded at last. "Will you miss me if I go?"

The question caught her off guard. Her eyes widened and her lips parted, but no words came out. Usually their exchanges hovered on the verge of personal without either of them crossing that line. Tonight, he'd changed the game by giving her a glimpse into what was bothering him, by trusting her with his plans for the future.

"I'll miss your business," she retorted with a wry smile that didn't quite reach her eyes. She uncrossed her legs, signaling their conversation was at an end.

"Violet." He caught her hand before she could rise. The casual contact created a complex chain reaction in JT's gut. He wanted her. That had never been in doubt. But what lay below the lust was dangerous beyond belief. "I'm really sorry about Tiberius."

He gave her hand a gentle squeeze and released her. It rattled him how hard it was to relax his fingers and set her free. What he wanted to do was draw her into his arms and let her soak the shoulder of his suit coat with her tears. He knew it was impossible. They didn't share that level of intimacy. The fact both relieved and frustrated him.

"Thank you." Two polite words, but her tone carried a wealth of emotion. She dabbed at the corner of her eye, catching teardrops on her knuckles. "I'm such a mess."

"I think you're beautiful."

Such a simple statement from such a complicated man. Unvarnished and without subtext, the words shook her. Needing a second to compose herself, Violet made quick apologies and headed for the bar to snag a couple of drink napkins to soak up her tears. Feeling steady once more, she returned to where JT now stood.

"Are you okay?"

The hard, unyielding businessman was back. As Violet nodded in response to his question, she breathed a sigh of relief. Whatever glimpse she'd had behind the curtain, however brief, made JT that much more interesting. And that was problematic.

Long ago she'd accepted that one look from him set her hormones off like Roman candles. Lust she could handle. She was a modern girl with a healthy appetite for sex. Maybe she didn't indulge often, but that didn't mean she wasn't interested. Just cautious.

It was the way her heart sped up whenever she spotted JT that concerned her. Getting romantic notions about a man as emotionally unavailable as JT would only lead to heartbreak. And she'd seen the effects of that sort of misery up close. Violet's mother had been abandoned by her married lover and left with a baby to support. Ross Fontaine had taken everything Lucille Allen had to give and moved on without a backward glance. Yet despite her heart being a shattered mess, Violet's mother still loved Ross and would to her dying day.

No. Violet was way too smart to end up like her mother. The instant the uncharitable thought surfaced, Violet regretted it. She loved her mom like crazy. It was just that being Lucille's daughter had forced Violet to grow up too fast. If not for Tiberius, she'd have had no childhood at all.

He'd adored Lucille. Taken on the responsibility for her and her daughter. They'd been his family. Not legally, of course, because even though he loved Lucille and wanted to marry her, she refused to give up on the hope that one day Ross Fontaine would return to her.

When Violet gave her heart, it would be to someone available, emotionally as well as legally. His reputation as a smart, fair businessman impressed the hell out of her, but when it came to personal relationships, he never went all in.

Not that he'd given her any reason to believe he thought of her as anything other than a competitor who'd stolen his favorite bartender. Tonight that had changed. Tonight he'd asked if she'd miss him if he left Las Vegas and made her believe his next heartbeat hinged on her saying that she would.

Violet brushed away her fanciful thoughts, but she couldn't ignore how her pulse had hitched at the gentle strength of his hand on hers. This was just simple desire. Nothing more. The man was six-feet, one-inch of rock solid male. Handsome with his black hair and bold eyebrows. The slight downturn of his chiseled lips. The fathomless ocean blue of his eyes.

Her instincts said he was a man who could use some help and she was a girl who loved cheering on her teammates. Only he wasn't on her team or even part of her circle. She would be wise to mind her own business where he was concerned. If she became too invested in offering him help that he did not want, she'd end up getting burned.

"I'd better get going or I'll be completely off schedule," she said, but couldn't bring her feet to move. Something had changed between them tonight and walking away from JT was proving difficult.

"I'd better get going as well," he told her, glancing at his watch. "If you need anything I hope you'll call."

More surprises. "Sure." She couldn't imagine what sort of help she'd turn to him for. Most of the time she was pretty self-sufficient. She'd had to be. Her mother was too easily overwhelmed by the least difficulty. Violet had learned to take care of herself from an early age, even when life had grown less challenging after they'd moved in with Tiberius when Violet was six. "That's nice of you."

For a brief moment his eyes softened. Before she could draw an unsteady breath he'd retreated behind his reserve once more.

"It's not being nice," he said, neutral and polite. "We're family."

His declaration was the cherry on top of a triple scoop sundae of surprises. "How do you figure?"

"It might not be the most traditional connection, but you were my uncle's daughter."

"Not legally." Violet wasn't sure how to cope with a connection of this sort with JT. If things became affectionate between them she might just step out of the neutral zone and into treacherous territory.

"Do you really think that mattered to Tiberius?"

"No." Violet cocked her head and regarded him. "But I would have thought it mattered to you."

"Why?"

Violet floundered. Confronting people didn't come naturally to her. It was a skill she'd worked hard to develop during her years in management positions and when she did speak her mind, it was after careful preparation.

But JT had flustered her tonight and she'd spoken without thought.

"The truth is I really don't know."

"But you had a reason to say it," he persisted, his interest laser-sharp.

Admitting her flaws wasn't something she did often, but Violet felt she owed JT an explanation after he'd been so kind to her tonight. "I didn't like growing up the bastard daughter of Ross Fontaine," she explained. "Being treated as if I didn't exist by the entire Fontaine family gave me a huge chip on my shoulder."

"That's changed now. Henry Fontaine not only welcomed you as his granddaughter, he gave you a hotel to run and a shot at becoming CEO of the family business."

Violet nodded. "And most days that amazes me. But sometimes I regress to that eleven-year-old girl who was ridiculed by her classmates for bragging that I was Ross Fontaine's daughter when everyone could tell he wanted nothing to do with me."

"I can see where that would be hard."

She had a difficult time believing JT could sympathize

with her situation. The sole heir to Stone Properties, he'd grown up knowing who he was and where he belonged. Maybe things hadn't been perfect with his parents and maybe the company was struggling with his father at the helm, but that could be turned around with the right moves.

"So, you think we're family," she said, aiming for a warm smile. She could tell by JT's expression that she missed the mark.

"I didn't have a chance to know my uncle," he explained. "I think I missed a lot. You knew him better than anyone. I feel connected to him through you."

It took a second for Violet to register that JT was reaching out to her. All of a sudden she felt a little giddy. "Your uncle was my father in all ways but legally." She sounded a tad breathless as she finished, "I suppose that makes us cousins."

JT cocked his head and regarded her. "I suppose it does. Good night, Violet."

He departed Baccarat without touching her again and Violet was dismayed by her disappointment. She could get used to having his hands on her. Was that creepy now that they'd agreed to consider each other cousins?

Violet continued on her rounds, and contemplated what her sisters would make of her conversation with JT. With her traditional upbringing and ambitious professional goals, Harper would give her sensible and conservative advice. Younger than Violet by a few months, Harper was nonetheless the voice of pragmatism. She would encourage Violet to keep her distance from a complicated man in a tricky family situation. Violet's relationship with Tiberius had made her by extension an enemy of Preston Rhodes, JT's father. If she and JT became friendly, it would only complicate what she sensed was a strained relationship with his father.

While Harper's rational arguments would appeal to Violet's head, Scarlett's opinion would go to work on her heart. A few weeks ago Scarlet had pointed out that there was more to JT's nightly appearance at Baccarat than simply that he missed Rick's mixology expertise. Scarlett would encourage Violet to get to know JT better; she was convinced that something would ignite between them. Shock waves pummeled Violet's midsection as her thoughts ventured down that path.

Sex with JT would be explosive. Tonight when he'd squeezed her hand, she'd been hard-pressed not to lean over and plant a very uncousinly kiss on his well-shaped lips. Her skin tingled at the thought and she gave her head a vigorous shake. She couldn't go there. Shouldn't even think about going there. Trouble was when she was around JT, she had a hard time thinking clearly.

Angst and passion simmered beneath his expensive suits and professional demeanor. During the six years she'd known him she'd occasionally caught glimpses of deep pain, and her instinct had been to offer comfort or help. But JT was a man who stubbornly resisted admitting to any vulnerability or weakness. From Tiberius, Violet knew JT's childhood hadn't been ideal. His father was a ruthless businessman who'd manipulated his father-in-law into disowning his only son. His drive for power had caused him to neglect his wife.

JT's mother had not taken the banishment of her brother well. She'd retreated into alcohol and pills. Tiberius had kept tabs on her through friends, but he'd been unable to do more than stand by and watch her fade away. What Violet had never understood is why she'd never divorced Preston. She might have had a chance at happiness if she had.

Violet finished her rounds and returned to her large executive office. Even though it was three in the morning, she didn't expect to sleep. Reports awaited her attention.

The hotel's management offices occupied a small chunk

of the third floor. She spent little time here, preferring to
be on the floor, eyes on the action taking place in her hotel.

It's what she'd learned from shadowing Tiberius around
the Lucky Heart. Her throat closed as she stared down the
Las Vegas strip to where the small hotel and casino sat.
Built in the sixties, it lacked the amenities of the modern hotels and casinos: five-star restaurants, extravagant
décor and luxury suites. The ceilings were low. The carpet
needed replacing. And the clientele came in for the cheap
bar drinks and stayed for the loose slots. But for Violet it
would always be home.

Which is why she'd been surprised how Tiberius had
reacted when Henry Fontaine approached her about coming to work for him. She'd expected Tiberius to discourage
her from joining the family business. Quite the opposite.
Tiberius knew how hard it had been for her to be Ross
Fontaine's bastard daughter. Unlike Scarlett, Ross's other
illegitimate daughter, Violet had grown up in Las Vegas
within the long shadow of the gorgeous hotels and casinos
that were owned by the Fontaine dynasty.

The older she got, the more being an outsider frustrated
her. Without Tiberius as her champion, constantly making
as if she was the smartest, most capable person he'd ever
known, she might never have accepted that she didn't need
approval from the Fontaines to make her happy.

Maybe that's why she sympathized with JT. If his
grandfather hadn't died when JT was ten, Preston would
never have taken over Stone Properties and ousted his
brother-in-law. The company would have stayed in Stone
hands. First Tiberius's, then JT's.

Attending his uncle's memorial service today must have
really upset him. She had no other explanation for why he'd
shared with her his concerns regarding Stone Properties.
They'd known each other for six years and as much as he
made her pulse dance, he'd always just treated her like a

business acquaintance. Was it any wonder his behavior to-night had thrown her off balance? Did he regret telling her about his worries for his family's company? It just wasn't like him to be so…forthcoming.

She smirked as she imagined him kicking himself the entire way back to Titanium.

It was a spectacular property. He'd spent his first two years in Vegas rebuilding the hotel and casino. It was larger than both Fontaine Chic and Richesse combined, with a huge convention facility and an eighteen-hole golf course in the back. Admiring the hotel's style, she'd used the same design company to bring to life her vision for Fontaine Chic.

What would happen to Stone Properties if JT left? As hurt as Tiberius had been that his father believed Preston's lies and disinherited him, Tiberius's biggest concern had always been for the company beneath Preston's steward-ship. He would be worried that JT was quitting.

"Not my problem," she muttered, but already the wheels were turning in her mind.

Tiberius would have wanted her to help JT. Despite all the years they'd been estranged, right before his death, Ti-berius had started reaching out to his nephew.

And Violet was confident she could keep her head screwed on straight and her hormones in check long enough to figure out a way to help JT save Stone Proper-ties. With the decision made, Violet headed to her suite for a hot shower and a good night's sleep.

Two

Violet stared at the shelves of law books that covered the walls of the lawyer's office, her eyes gritty and dry. In contrast, her mother sat beside her, weeping softly. In the weeks since Tiberius's death, Lucille had gone through a dozen boxes of tissues.

A part of Violet was ashamed that she'd moved swiftly through the five stages of grief while her mother had gone straight to stage four—depression—and stayed there.

"That takes us to the Lucky Heart," John Malcolm, Tiberius's lawyer continued. "As you probably know, the casino is deep in debt."

Violet nodded, absently squeezing her mother's hand in comfort, relieved that Tiberius had invested his personal fortune wisely and set aside enough for Lucille to never have to worry about money. "I don't understand why. The entire time I worked there, it always operated in the black. Nor has business fallen off in the last five years. Tiberius was too savvy to let that happen. So where did the debt come from?"

"He was mortgaging the Lucky Heart in order to buy stock."

"Stock?" That didn't sound like Tiberius at all. "Why would he do that? He didn't trust Wall Street. Said it was a sucker's bet."

"He was buying private stock."

Even more curious. A rhythmic ache had manifested in Violet's temples. She rubbed to ease the pain. "So can we sell the stock and get the Lucky Heart out of debt?"

"Unfortunately, you're not going to be able to do that."

"Why not?" Making bad business decisions was something Tiberius had never done. "What sort of stock was he buying?"

"Stone Properties stock."

Violet leaned forward. Had she heard the gray-haired lawyer correctly? "Why would he do that?"

John's solemn blue eyes were the gatekeepers of a thousand clients' secrets. "He had his reasons."

Her thoughts rushed through a dozen scenarios as to why Tiberius had kept something this huge from her. Then she contemplated her conversation with JT a few days earlier. "How much stock did he have?"

"In the three months before his death he'd managed to get eighteen percent."

Violet's curiosity spiked. Did his purchase of Stone Properties stock have anything to do with why he'd been reestablishing his relationship with JT? Together they would've controlled forty-eight percent of Stone Properties, not enough to take over and force Preston out, but if they could secure another three percent…

Is that what Tiberius had been up to?

"Did he leave the stock to JT?"

John Malcolm looked surprised. "No. He left it to you."

Any normal person who'd just inherited eighteen percent of a multi-billion dollar company might be dancing around the lawyer's office or at the very least grinning. Violet had no desire to celebrate. The price tag for her windfall was too high. She'd lost the man who'd been her father in heart and soul if not by blood or marriage.

"Why me and not my mom?"

"Because he trusted you'd know what to do with it."

"First Scarlett inherits a warehouse full of secret files and now this," she muttered, thinking about all the private information Tiberius had gathered over the years on acquaintances and family. "What other surprises does Tiberius plan to unleash on the Fontaine sisters?"

"Now, as to the conditions of the inheritance."

"And there it is," Violet grumbled. She loved Tiberius, but he was a cagey bastard.

John Malcolm ignored her outburst. "You can't sell the stock, donate it or give it away." The lawyer smiled ironically as he said this last bit, if he couldn't understand why anyone could part with that much money and expect nothing in return. "Until the death of Preston Rhodes."

Obviously Tiberius wanted to make sure his brother-in-law never got his hands on the stock.

"Chances are it won't be worth anything by the time that happens," she murmured.

"And there's one other issue," John Malcolm continued as if she hadn't spoken. "You can't vote the shares because you're not family."

Violet sat back in her chair and regarded the lawyer in utter bafflement. Why hadn't Tiberius just left the shares to JT? The answer occurred to her an instant after the question had formed. Because his relationship with JT hadn't reached that level of trust yet. Tiberius probably thought he had months to get to know his nephew. It wasn't like he was planning on getting murdered.

"Thank you for all your help," Violet said, standing to shake hands with the lawyer.

"Yes," Lucille echoed. "Thank you. I know you were a good friend to Tiberius all these years."

"Sometimes I felt more like a co-conspirator," John Malcolm with a wry smile. "But it was my pleasure to call him both friend and client."

Violet and her mother left the lawyer's office and headed to the parking lot.

"I can't believe Tiberius left you all that stock," Lucille said, "without there being anything you can do with it."

"Did he talk to you about what he was up to?"

Lucille's beautiful smile was always a little bit sad, but since Tiberius's death it had become downright melancholy. "You know he didn't talk business with me."

No. Tiberius had always made it his mission to bring all things joyful and fun to his conversations with Lucille. He'd loved when her eyes sparkled. Discussing something as upsetting as staging a coup against Preston Rhodes would never have happened.

"Maybe I'll check his office when I drop you off," Violet said.

"There might be something in his files."

When they arrived at the house Lucille had shared with Tiberius for years, Violet discovered that her mother was right. There were ten files pertaining to the stock acquisition. Two contained the paperwork for the stock Tiberius had purchased. The other eight contained information on family members he hadn't yet contacted. Her interest rose as she read through Tiberius's notes. Gaining another three percent wouldn't be easy, but she had a notion of how it could be done. Not that it did her any good. She owned eighteen percent of a stock she could neither get rid of nor vote.

So, what the hell was she supposed to do with it? Better to ask, what would Tiberius want her to do with it?

The thought of becoming embroiled in the intrigue surrounding Stone Properties gave Violet a bad taste in her mouth. She was quite content with her own piece of the

Las Vegas strip. From the second she'd been put in charge of Fontaine Chic, she'd known complete happiness. It was all she needed. She didn't care if she won the contest their grandfather had created to decide which of the three Fontaine sisters would succeed him as CEO. Violet was realistic about her chances. With Harper's education and hotel training, it was her contest hands down. Besides, it was her birthright. Just like Stone Properties was JT's.

If only there was something Violet could do to make it so he could claim his rightful place. Not that he wanted her help. She dismissed that as insignificant. She needed to focus on keeping alive Tiberius's plan to reclaim his family's company. But how?

When the answer came, she was stunned by its simplicity and foolhardiness. She couldn't. The idea was crazy. On the other hand, maybe crazy was what the situation called for.

And there was only one way she was going to know for sure.

JT was about to leave his usual spot in Baccarat and head back to his hotel when he spotted Violet approaching the bar. Tension he'd not been aware of released its grip on his muscles. He relaxed his clenched teeth and felt a scowl melt from his forehead.

Since finding out what his father had been up to with Stone Properties, he'd been frustrated and in great need of a confidante he could trust. He trusted Violet. Sharing his problems with her had eased his mind.

For the last five days she'd been absent from the lounge. Either she'd been detained by hotel business or she'd been avoiding him. Thinking she might be avoiding him had been a bitter pill to swallow.

He'd stepped across the line at their last meeting. Claiming her as family had pushed their association past the boundaries of casual acquaintances. But no matter how much it worried him that he might become dependent on her, he couldn't stop craving her support.

To his unreasonable delight, the instant she entered the bar, her gaze sought his and she immediately headed his way. As she drew near, the spicy scent of her perfume preceded her and he had just enough time to draw a heady lungful before she sat beside him. Tonight's black dress was a knee-length sheath with a deep scoop neckline that showed off the upper curves of her breasts. Keeping his attention on her face proved challenging as she gathered a deep breath before speaking.

"I'm glad you're here tonight," she said, her voice brisk, expression resolute.

He resisted the urge to remind her that he was here every night. She already had him eating out of the palm of her hand. Why give her more power?

"You look beautiful," he told her, letting his gaze drift over her.

His compliment caused her to blink. "Thank you." For a moment she looked as if she'd lost her train of thought.

Despite the bar's low light, he spied a rush of color in her cheeks and noticed an uneven hitch to her breath. In that instant he realized she'd felt the impact of his attraction for her, even if she wasn't ready to admit it.

The revelation inspired a rush of longing to touch her smooth skin, to pull her body tight to his and hear her sigh beneath his lips. He imagined sweeping his tongue across her breasts and hearing her cry out. Not seeing her these last few days had fueled his hunger for her. He'd spent far too much time pondering exactly how he would make love to her.

"JT, are you listening to me?"

He shook his head and dispelled the evocative images

lingering there. "Sorry. I was distracted. Is that a new perfume you're wearing?"

"It's something Tiberius gave to my mother last Christmas. Since his death she can't bear to wear it, but I love the scent so she gave me the bottle."

"It's nice," he murmured.

"Thank you." She paused and regarded him through narrowed eyes. "We went to Tiberius's lawyer for the reading of his will a couple days ago."

JT wrestled his libido back under control as her words registered. "And he left everything to you and your mother."

"Yes." She scowled at him as if he was supposed to comprehend a deeper meaning to what she'd said. "But it's *what* he left that caught me by surprise."

"His house, bank accounts, the hotel." JT ticked the items off on his fingers. "What else?"

A smug grin bloomed on her full lips. "How about eighteen percent of Stone Properties stock."

The news dealt him a sturdy blow. "How did he get it?"

"He mortgaged the Lucky Heart and bought every share he could."

"But why?"

"To take on your father?"

"Eighteen percent wouldn't do him any good. When my mother died she left my father thirty percent of the company. Combined with the rest of what my family owns, he has enough votes to control the company."

"Until two months ago when you turned thirty. Your father controlled your trust fund until then, didn't he?"

"Yes." JT didn't know what to make of what he was hearing. "You think my uncle wanted us to join forces?" He recalled the dinners Tiberius had invited him to. "He never said anything of the sort."

"I think he wanted to get to know you before he committed to anything."

For the first time in years JT felt a flutter of excitement. Combining what he'd inherited with Violet's shares left him three percent away from taking the company back from his father and repairing all the damage that had been done.

"How much do you want for your stock?"

Violet had been watching him closely, grinning at his reaction to her news, but now delight drained from her expression. "That's where things get a little tricky."

Suspicion flared before JT remembered that this was Violet he was dealing with. She was loyal and a team player. She wasn't here to get something from him. She honestly wanted to help. But none of his trust reflected in his tone as he asked, "Tricky how?"

"The terms of Tiberius's will don't allow me to sell, trade or donate the shares in any way." She looked as if she expected him to explode in frustration. "Otherwise you have to know, I'd let you have them."

Although disappointed by his uncle's unorthodox terms, JT knew there was a way he could work this to his advantage. "But you can give me your proxy vote." Of course, he only had eighteen percent, but if Tiberius had convinced several of their family members to part with the stock, surely that meant JT could do the same. He only needed three percent more.

"That's the other problem," she said, apology in her tone. "The way your grandfather set up the stock, only family members by blood or by marriage can vote. Since, I'm not family, my votes can't count."

JT exhaled in exasperation. "So we're back to square one. With your votes voided, my father remains in control of the majority of the stock."

But Tiberius's plan was still a viable option. JT and

his father each had thirty percent of the shares. With Violet's eighteen percent excluded, that left twenty-two percent up for grabs. If he could buy twelve percent of the shares belonging to the rest of the family or failing that, convince them to swing their votes his way, he could take the company back.

"Not back to square one," Violet said, interrupting his train of thought. "If I was family, I could vote the shares."

"If you were family, yes," JT agreed, his gaze fixed on the lights racing around above the bar. "But you're not."

"I could be."

Something in her tone caught his attention. A tentative smile trembled at the corners of her lips. She was trying to tell him something, but his mind was darting in too many directions to grasp the nuances of her meaning.

"How?"

"We could get married."

If she'd nailed him with a cattle prod he couldn't have been more stunned. "Married?"

"In name only, of course." She offered him a cheeky grin that didn't reach her eyes. "There's nothing in my uncle's will that prevents me from marrying the shares away."

"Since he knew we'd never get married, it probably never crossed his mind."

She cocked her head and regarded him solemnly. "And how did he know something like that?"

"I told him I had no intention of starting anything up with you."

Violet sat up very straight. Her eyes narrowed. "You two talked about me?"

JT nodded. "When I first arrived in town. Tiberius had heard about my activities in Miami and was worried that if I pursued you, you might get hurt. I agreed to keep my distance."

"How noble." Her tone dripped with scorn.

"Not that noble," he retorted, deciding if they were going to consider her wild scheme, she might as well hear the whole truth. "It was an easy promise to make. You really aren't my type."

Mouth tight, she stared at him for several seconds. But then her hand stole across his leg, mid-thigh, and lingered.

"You aren't my type either." But her husky tone and the come-get-me-big-boy look in her eyes said the exact opposite. "So that should make a marriage in-name-only a snap."

JT kept his expression bland. No need for her to learn the truth. He'd promised himself that nothing would happen between them. He needed her in his corner far more than he needed her naked in his bed. He wasn't about to ruin their fledgling connection over something as fleeting as lust.

"It should." But he didn't feel as confident as he sounded. "And it isn't forever."

"Right. We only need to be married long enough for me to vote my shares at the annual meeting. It's at the end of August, right?"

"August twenty-fifth."

"That's only six weeks away."

JT had another thought. "Your family isn't going to be happy if you marry me without some sort of a prenup."

"At the moment I'm not worth more than the stock I inherited from Tiberius and what I've saved towards retirement. We can sign a simple agreement that states we leave the marriage with what we arrived with."

She made everything sound so reasonable. So why was he resisting?

Sure, marriage wasn't on his to-do list. He enjoyed playing the part of confirmed bachelor. Las Vegas was the perfect place to find attractive, single women looking for a little fun. They came in for a weekend and he gave them the royal treatment. Then they were gone. No fuss. No muss.

Violet was a whole different package. She was in Vegas to stay. Getting involved with her would be complicated and undoubtedly end in heartbreak. His.

But it wasn't as if they were getting married for real. He just needed to remember that.

"So are we going to do this?" She'd plucked her palm from his thigh, leaving behind a distracting tingle.

"You're sure you want to marry me?" His heart thumped hard against his ribs as he reminded himself this was a business deal.

"Want to marry you? Absolutely not." Her lighthearted laugh had a slightly wicked edge. "But I feel like I owe it to Tiberius to finish what he started. And I'd like to see you take back your family's company."

He scrutinized her lovely features, finding only altruism in her expression. Her self-sacrifice made him uncomfortable.

"I get that you feel an obligation to Tiberius, but I'm not sure this is the best idea."

"I don't feel obligated."

From her earnest expression he could tell she didn't. And that's what worried JT the most.

"Okay, but you're also looking for a way to make your shares pay off too, right?"

She cocked her head and regarded him in silence for several seconds. "You yourself said the company isn't doing well with your father at the helm. If he continues, the shares will lose value. Maybe even become worthless. I know you'll make a much better CEO. I'm protecting myself the best way I can."

Her answer rang with conviction. JT's resistance eased minutely. Still, he should refuse. The only way this wasn't going to backfire on them both was if he turned down her help. But the idea of getting that much closer to Violet was a temptation of the hard-to-resist variety.

But marriage? Was the opportunity to rescue Stone Properties from his father's clutches worth the danger of getting too attached to Violet? He already liked her far too much for his own good. Watching her walk into the lounge was enough to make his day. What if he started to rely on spending lots of time with her? He knew himself well enough to know that just being friends wouldn't cut it. He wanted her. Badly. It was only a matter of time before he did something about it.

After a fast and furious debate, JT kicked self-preservation to the curb.

"Then I'm in." He was on the verge of getting on one knee and proposing to her properly when she spoke up.

"I think we should do this sooner rather than later. Before either one of us comes to our senses."

"How soon?" She'd saved him from going all romantic—even if it was just for show—and making an ass out of himself. "Like Saturday?"

"What about now?" Seeing his shock, she rushed on. "Too fast?"

"A little." But what the hell. If they waited, the anticipation might prompt him to do something stupid. Like let her see how badly he needed her. "But it's doable. Your chapel or mine?"

"How about someplace neutral. The Tunnel of Love Chapel?"

Some of JT's tension faded. She really was approaching this as a business arrangement and he needed to do so as well. But ignoring her effect on him was easier said than done.

"Positively romantic," he said, his tone dry.

"Good." She glanced at her phone. "I booked it for midnight."

"You were feeling pretty confident I'd say yes."

She shrugged. "It made perfect business sense that you would."

But business was the furthest thing from his thoughts at the moment. He was contemplating all the delightful things a husband did with his brand-new wife. "Are you going to leave the booking of the honeymoon suite to me?"

She looked positively horrified. "Perhaps I wasn't very clear. A marriage in name only means no sex."

"Not even on our wedding night?" he couldn't resist asking. She was so delightfully earnest. It made teasing her a pleasure.

"I thought I wasn't your type." Her voice lacked any trace of amusement.

"Since you're going to be my wife," he said, "I figured I should make an exception just this once."

"It's a lovely thought but we should really keep this all business between us."

"Whatever you say."

"It will make things easier."

She was oh so wrong about that. Nothing about being married to Violet was going to be easy. In fact, he'd better brace himself because things were about to get a whole lot harder.

Three

On her way across Fontaine Chic's lobby, Violet decided it was okay if a bride felt excited and slightly terrified on her wedding day. Especially if the groom was sexy and enigmatic and the decision to marry was somewhere between logically conceived and wildly impulsive.

Wearing an off-white lace dress she'd bought on impulse that morning from one of the hotel's shops, Violet's heart double-timed to each click of her heels on the black marble floor. She clutched an overnight bag and a briefcase filled with Tiberius's files on the holders of Stone Properties stock. Against her better judgment, she'd let JT talk her into spending their wedding night together at his house. In separate bedrooms, of course.

She wasn't worried that he'd take advantage of her. He'd already pointed out that she wasn't his type. That declaration still stung. With his reputation as a player, she hadn't suspected he had a type beyond female, single and young. She was all those. So what about her didn't appeal to him?

Was she the wrong height? Too thin? Too fat? Not pretty enough? Not sexy?

Violet slammed the door on curiosity. It didn't matter if she was his type or not. Their marriage was a business arrangement. She needed to remember that. And to guard against demonstrating the way her body came alive whenever he drew near.

A bright blue BMW convertible stood at the ready in the hotel's circular driveway. JT leaned against the car's hood, wearing a dark gray, almost black suit and white shirt with a blush-colored tie that emphasized his potent charisma. He hadn't spotted her yet so she had a private moment to observe his relaxed posture and utter gorgeousness as he joked with one of her bellhops. Thanks to anxiety, her muscles hadn't been responding properly to the signals from her brain for the last hour; now they were positively spastic.

He was still laughing when their gazes met. The power of his smile knocked the breath from her lungs. Wanting his eyes to light up with pleasure at seeing her, she was crushed at how fast he sobered.

"Right on time, I see." He stepped forward to take her bags.

Was he used to waiting for the women he dated? They probably took longer to primp and fuss than she had. In truth, her nerves had prevented her from applying eyeliner with a steady hand so she'd just dusted her lids with neutral eye shadow, buffed her cheekbones with blush and used a little powder to keep down the shine. It didn't occur to her that she hadn't applied lipstick until his gaze locked on her mouth.

A bride shouldn't attend her wedding in such a state. She dug in her purse, but all she found was some lip balm. "Damn," she muttered. "I don't have any lipstick."

"You don't need any." He opened the passenger door for her and gave her plenty of room to get by him. It was almost as if he was avoiding her. But why would he need to do that?

"I'm not sure I feel completely dressed without it."

"I assure you, you're completely dressed."

Was that humor she saw in his expression? Oh how she wished she could read his mind. It would be nice to know how the man she was about to marry thought, but it wasn't likely to happen now, or ever. He would make certain of that.

"I wonder what else I forgot to pack," she mused, her brain on autopilot. "I had some last-minute things to take care of with my assistant. I was afraid I was going to be late."

"And that I might change my mind?"

"The thought occurred to me." She slid into her seat and watched him circle the car. "What about you? Did you think I might chicken out?"

"No. I think you are the most dependable person I know." His statement made it sound as if he knew more about her than their limited association had led her to believe. He slipped behind the wheel and started the engine.

Violet regarded his strong profile, admiring the precise cut of his jaw and his ridiculously long eyelashes. "What makes you say that?"

"From your reputation around town. Whenever you make a commitment to a cause or a promise to a friend you come through. No matter what."

As the car rolled toward South Las Vegas Boulevard, Violet put her hands to her cheeks and found them hot with embarrassment. "I don't do more than anyone else."

"And then you rarely take credit for all the good things you do." The light turned green as they approached it and JT was able to turn onto the strip without stopping. "It causes people to take advantage of your generosity."

Was he trying to warn her that this is what he was

doing? If he was, it was too late. She was already committed to their goal.

"You make me sound like a sap."

"I was trying to pay you a compliment."

"A backhanded one, maybe. *You're a dependable door-mat*." She made a face. "That's a fine way to talk about your bride-to-be."

An impatient sound erupted from him. "In the future I'll remember that flattery makes you prickly."

"See that you do. I prefer honesty to sweet talk." She stared at him in silence until he'd stopped at a light and looked her way. "Are you going to have a problem with that?"

"Not at all."

"Good. Just think of me as a fellow businessperson and we'll get along just fine."

JT merely nodded his agreement.

Ten minutes later, they swung into the Tunnel of Love Chapel. It wasn't Violet's first trip through the tunnel. Her best friend from high school had tied the knot here the day after graduation and two short months before baby Cory was born. JT, however, looked like he'd never seen anything like the blue ceiling adorned with cupids and stars.

He stopped the car before a booth with a sign that read "The Little White Wedding Chapel Drive Thru Window," and they filled out the paperwork for the marriage license. Getting married in Las Vegas was a simple matter. Maybe too simple? Time for second thoughts came and went in the blink of an eye. As the opening words of the wedding ceremony began, a strange buzzing filled her ears.

Was she really marrying JT Stone? Violet glanced from the man framed by the booth window to JT. Her lips twitched uncontrollably. As first JT then she repeated the vows spoken by the minister, Violet was overwhelmed by the dreamlike aspect of her wedding. She didn't feel attached to the body sitting in the car beside JT. And she didn't recognize her voice promising to love and honor him. It wasn't until JT pulled out two platinum rings and she felt the cold metal slide onto her finger that she crashed back to earth.

She had only a second to scrutinize her ring's antique setting. The setting was square, the diamond round, the corners filled in with ornate filigree. Violet guessed the stone to be over two and a half carats. Smaller round diamonds flanked the center stone. He slipped the ring on her left hand. The instant she realized it fit, all her agitation disappeared and she was struck by the rightness of what she was doing.

The minister interrupted her thoughts. "Now the bride."

JT handed her the other ring, this one embossed with waves and swirls. Repeating the vows that symbolized love and commitment, Violet slipped the ring onto JT's finger. She couldn't look him in the eye. Her wild idea to marry JT so she could use her stock to put him in charge of his family's company was on the verge of becoming legally and morally binding.

"I now pronounce you man and wife," the minister proclaimed.

Violet's heart had been erratic since JT had agreed to marry her. Now it was positively aflutter. They'd done it. For good or for bad, there was no going back.

"You may kiss the bride."

Mouth dry, Violet waited for her first kiss from JT. Her stomach had been in knots for the last several hours since they'd agreed to get married. How would he kiss her? Would it be passionate? Romantic? Would he sweep her into his arms and steal her breath or would he woo her with slow, sensual kisses? Either way, she knew it would be perfect.

She'd never dreamed he'd catch her chin in his fingers and plant a quick kiss at the corner of her lips. Lost in a fog of disappointment, she automatically went through the formalities that followed and accepted the congratulations of the witnesses with a heavy heart.

And then the car was rolling out of the Tunnel of Love Chapel and emerging into the noise and lights of Las Vegas once more. While JT negotiated the traffic on his way to the freeway, Violet stared at the ring on her hand. How had he gotten a set of wedding rings on such short notice? And such unique ones at that.

"It's my grandmother's," JT said as if reading her mind. "And this is my grandfather's." He held up his left hand. "I drove to the ranch before picking you up."

Rendered speechless at the significance of wearing a family heirloom, Violet gaped at him. Harper would laugh at her for believing that jewelry held the energy of the wearer, but what else could explain the tranquility that came over her the instant she'd put on his grandmother's ring? They'd married without love. She didn't deserve to be wearing something so dear.

"Is something wrong?" he prompted.

"We could have bought rings at the chapel."

"Why, when these were collecting dust in my safe?"

"But it's your grandmother's ring."

He eyed her. "And I trust that as soon as it's no longer necessary, you'll return it."

"Of course." It was beginning to annoy her that he wasn't getting the significance of the jewelry he'd just pledged his troth with. Heaving a sigh, Violet decided to let it drop. In a few months it would be back in his safe where it belonged.

As the car streaked through the Nevada night, the adrenaline rush she'd been riding for the last two days began to fade. Her confidence waned as well. She was now married to a man who was for all intents and purposes a virtual stranger. And with the strength of his deflector shields, he was likely to stay that way no matter how delicately she probed. Which she really shouldn't do.

What she had to remember was that despite the marriage vows they'd just exchanged, theirs was a union of expediency. Mutual benefit. JT got the chance to reclaim his family's business. She would finish what Tiberius had started and preserve the stock's value.

It was a business arrangement. He would resist her efforts to dig around in his private thoughts in an attempt to get to know him better.

"Now what's bothering you?" JT quizzed.

"Nothing, why?"

For the last half hour they'd been heading north out of town on I-25. His sixty-acre ranch sat just beyond the outskirts of the city. At first she'd resisted being away from the hotel on such short notice, but since Tiberius's death, she'd been working herself hard and could really use a night off.

"You haven't said a word in fifteen minutes," JT said. "It's not like you."

"Was it crazy, what we just did?"

"Completely." He exited the freeway and turned left onto a two-lane highway. "Have you changed your mind?"

"No." And she was surprised at how strongly she felt about staying the course. "It's all going to work out. We just need to get the last three percent Tiberius had been working on before the next stockholders' meeting."

JT nodded. "One way or another, we can be divorced before fall."

Her stomach fell at his eagerness to be rid of her and she chided herself for reacting so foolishly. That was the deal they'd made. She had no right to wish for something else.

"Then we'd better get to work immediately," she said. "I brought all the files from his desk at the house. He was about to approach eight more shareholders. Four of the leads look promising."

"I'll look at them first thing in the morning."

His use of first person singular wasn't lost on her. Before she returned to Fontaine Chic tomorrow, she was determined to make him understand that this undertaking was going to be a team effort. She'd married him and was determined he would not do battle with his father alone.

"This is going to work, you know."

He shot her a dour look. "Are you always this optimistic?"

"You make it sound like a bad thing."

"It's not bad, but I'm not sure it's realistic. Don't you ever worry?"

"Not about the future." She lifted her face to the wind streaming off the windshield. "Why bother? It's a blank slate, full of possibilities."

He didn't reply and she tried to be comfortable in the silence that filled the space between them once more. But the unfinished conversation itched like a case of hives.

"All the brooding you do in the bar every night. Tell me what good it does you to worry about things that haven't happened?"

"It's not the future that concerns me, but the past. Things I'd like to take back, do differently, but can't."

Delighted that JT was on the verge of a revelation, she prompted, "Such as?"

"Nothing I feel like talking about."

And just like that she was shut down. Violet heaved a sigh and lapsed into silence. What a puzzle he was. She knew his childhood hadn't been one to brag about. His father's ambition. His mother's retreat into alcohol and drugs. Emotional injuries he'd suffered at a fragile age had turned him into a wild teenager. When JT had first arrived in Las Vegas, Tiberius had warned her to stay away from him. He was not a bird with a broken wing or a kitten who'd been struck by a car. He was a grown man who only knew how to use people and cast them aside.

Tiberius's initial opinion of his nephew had been right on, but Violet suspected it wasn't the whole picture. Curious about the Stone family, she'd conducted an internet search and discovered what sorts of trouble a party boy from Miami could get into. Although her contact with him had been limited these last six years, she didn't think he was the type to act out without cause. But whatever motivated him was locked deep inside and given the firm set of his jaw, likely to remain so.

"So you have a hard time letting go," she said. "How can you think that's good for you?"

"Reliving past events helps me avoid similar situations in my future."

When Violet considered her life, she decided she could probably spend a little time learning from her experiences. How many men had she dated who'd needed her to be their cheerleader or their psychologist or their financial advisor or their life coach? Too many. And here she was doing it again. Only this time she'd gone too far and had actually married someone.

JT turned down a long driveway bordered by landscape lighting and stopped the car in front of a massive stucco-and-stone prairie-style house. Curved planting beds held desert plants and tropical flowers. Their round lines softened the home's square architecture.

"This is definitely worth the commute," Violet said as she exited the car. The covered walkway to the front door was flanked by pillars covered in square stone and lighted by sconces. The effect was elegant and welcoming. "I can't get over how quiet it is." For a girl who'd practically grown up on the strip, the silence was a bit unnerving.

"Wait until morning. The view from the living room is what sold me on the property." He collected her bag from the trunk and gestured for her to precede him toward the front door.

The house continued to impress Violet as JT gave her a quick tour. From the expansive two-story foyer he led her into the combination living room-dining room. Such large spaces could seem cold and uninviting, but the coved ceilings, inset lighting and desert tones made it very homey. In the living room, sliding glass walls opened out onto a wide patio. The gourmet kitchen was almost as large as her suite at the hotel and contained all restaurant-quality appliances as well as a large wine chiller.

"I wish I knew how to cook," Violet said, gliding her palm along the center island's cool granite.

"You don't?" JT had fetched a bottle of champagne and a couple of glasses. He popped the cork and filled both flutes.

Violet accepted the champagne he handed her. "Just the basics. Not well enough to do justice to all this." She was proud of herself for standing her ground as JT stepped into her space and held up his glass.

Finding out that Tiberius had left her the stock. Her wild proposition to JT. The quick drive-through wedding that followed. And now, being alone with JT in his house. So much had happened. She was feeling a little exposed and emotional. Primed to do something stupid like demand a far better kiss than the one he'd deposited on her in the Tunnel of Love.

"To our successful merger," JT declared, touching his flute to hers. Crystal chimed in the large room.

"To getting Stone Properties away from your father." Violet drank sparingly. The man before her was a heady concoction. She didn't need to add alcohol to the mix.

"It's after one. Do you want me to show you to your room?"

"So I can do what?" Violet quizzed, walking toward the breakfast nook's bay windows. "Pace for hours? I don't know about you, but I rarely get to bed before three." She spied a turquoise pool behind the house. "Can I use that?"

"As of twelve-fifteen the house became half yours. You don't need to ask."

Violet gasped, all thoughts of a moonlit swim forgotten. "Oh, no. That's not what we agreed to. And when we get divorced, we'll just go our separate ways—I don't want half of your house."

"Maybe we should renegotiate our deal. I might need to demand alimony in the divorce settlement."

"Why would you need alimony?"

"Because if our plan fails my father will surely kick me out of the family business and the way he's running things, the stock won't be worth much." He leaned back against the counter and crossed his arms over his chest. "While you will be worth millions as Fontaine's CEO."

Because she couldn't tell if he was poking fun at her or not, Violet refrained from commenting on her chances of winning her grandfather's contest. "I never imagined that I would end up supporting you," she replied. "Perhaps we should get an annulment—"

"While we still can?" JT interrupted, his silky voice spreading shivers along her skin.

"Stop kidding around." She tried for lightness, but a hint of anxiety crept into her tone. "Just because we're married and alone in this house on our wedding night…" Violet trailed off. What point was she trying to make?

"Doesn't mean that we'll fall prey to our basic urges," JT finished.

"Exactly."

"Even if those urges are fueled by champagne and curiosity?"

Violet set her glass down and dismay sparked when she realized it was empty. "I think it's time you show me the bedroom. My bedroom," she corrected, feeling her cheeks heat. "Where I'm going to sleep. Alone."

JT picked up her bag and gestured back the way they'd come. "It's upstairs."

Violet attributed her lightheadedness to the champagne, refusing to believe that she was overwhelmed by the thought of spending the night alone with JT in his house. Was his room way down the hall from hers or a convenient few steps away?

Get a grip. You're not a virgin at your first frat party. You're a successful businesswoman and this man is a colleague. Keep your head and everything will be fine.

"Here you are." JT opened a door and gestured her inside. The large room contained a queen-size bed with matching cherry nightstands, a triple dresser, and a small seating area in front of a gas fireplace. He set her overnight bag on the bed and returned to where she stood just inside the bedroom door.

"This is nice. Thank you."

"I'm the one who should be thanking you. If this wild idea of yours works, I'll be able to save my family's company. And that's a debt I can't repay." JT leaned down and kissed her gently on the cheek. "Good night, Violet. I'll make sure I have green tea ready for you in the morning."

He knew that she didn't drink coffee? She vaguely recalled having a tea versus coffee discussion with him long ago. And he'd remembered.

"That's nice of you. And one more thing." Before she considered the wisdom of her actions, Violet lifted on tiptoe and coasted her palms along JT's massive shoulders. Shoving aside rational thought, she tunneled her fingers into his hair and murmured, "You didn't give me a proper kiss at our wedding."

"Then let me rectify that right now." He lowered his lips to hers.

Her breath stopped. Every nerve in her body screamed to life. Newly sensitized, her skin prickled at the slide of his cotton shirt against her bare arm as he cupped the side of her head to hold her in place. His lips were firm, but softer than she'd expected. The friction of his mouth on hers dragged a moan from her chest.

The sound spurred him to intensify the pressure of his kiss, but he retreated before she could act on her rising passion. His teeth caught at her tender flesh and gently tugged. She arched her back, seeking closer contact. This was so much better than she'd ever imagined.

He flattened his palm against her back, locking her in place before treating her to the first delicious lick of his tongue. A slow thrust followed. Warm. Wet. Skilled. He claimed her mouth as if he'd done it a thousand times. Taking his time, he explored every corner of her mouth, tantalizing her with his leashed passion. What happened if his control snapped? Violet was fast losing her wits. Much longer and her stance on a sexless marriage would topple.

Anticipation built as his hands coasted over her ribs, thumbs whisking provocatively over the outside curves of her breasts. She pulsed with need, craving his possession, and shifted restlessly against him to ease the ache.

JT tore his lips from hers and gulped air into his lungs. "Better?"

Better? Glorious was more like it.

Chest heaving, knees like pudding, she blinked to clear her vision and was startled to see they hadn't moved from the doorway. How was that possible when he'd turned her entire world upside down?

"Now I feel married," she said.

"You'd feel even more so after a proper wedding night," he murmured, letting his lips graze temptingly close to hers once more.

Unsure whether he was serious or merely taunting her, Violet clutched at his strong shoulders and leaned back in order to survey his expression. With eyes that glittered, JT probed her gaze. His compelling curiosity alarmed her. What was he looking for? Proof that his kisses rendered her insensible?

He swept his hands down her spine, fanned his fingers against the small of her back. Ever so slowly he pressed her hips forward, easing her against the hard length of him. Violet's legs trembled. She wanted nothing more than to be filled by him. To lose herself in his evocative touch.

Damn. She never should have asked for that kiss. If she'd just ignored the tension building between them, her body wouldn't be throbbing with unfulfilled longing nor would she be fighting temptation at the idea of one night with him. One incredible, mind-blowing night.

"JT, I…"

Before she figured out what she intended to say, shutters dropped over his gaze and she was left staring at an insurmountable wall. The speed with which he'd shut her out acted like a bucket of ice water on her overheated hormones.

"You don't need to explain." He relaxed his hold on her and stepped away. A sardonic smile tugged at his lips. "I know our marriage is only for show."

And she'd been seconds away from forgetting that fact. Humiliation chased away any lingering traces of desire. No question, she'd just dodged a bullet. So why was she so miserable about it?

"It's not that," she began and then frowned. "Well, it's mostly that, but the truth is, I don't know you very well and I'm not in the habit of falling into bed with a man this quickly."

"You know more about me than most of the women I date."

Really? Did that somehow elevate her above the numerous women that passed through his life? She bit her lip, disturbed by the yearning to be more than just another of his conquests. That was a dangerous road to travel. Better that they keep things all business between them.

"It'll just be easier if we keep everything strictly hands off." Who was she trying to convince, herself or him?

"Then I suggest you refrain from asking me to kiss you in the future." His icy tone was meant as a reproach, but Violet had tasted more than passion in his kiss. Or was she merely hoping that was the case?

"It was one kiss." She heard the defensive ring of her voice and dug her nails into her palms. "What's the big deal?"

"The big deal—" a muscle jumped in his jaw "—is that when I start something like what just happened between us, I like to finish it."

Why was he so exasperated? Not because she'd turned him down. Surely women had said no before. Hadn't they? "Haven't you ever kissed a woman without expecting to sleep with her?"

"Not since high school."

If he was trying to annoy her with his self-satisfied smirk, he was doing a fine job. "So, are you saying you don't bother to kiss a woman unless you're going to have sex with her?"

"I'm saying after I kiss a woman, she rarely says no to having sex with me."

This was so obviously a declaration of JT's reality that Violet crossed her arms over her chest and scowled. "Then I'm thrilled to be included in that minority of your female acquaintances."

"You forget that you are not one of my acquaintances. You are my wife."

JT took possession of her left hand and lifted it to eye level. His grandmother's ring caught the overhead light and sparkled. He couldn't explain why he was so angry with her at this moment. Could it be the unrelenting desire rumbling through him? Going to bed alone and horny was not how he'd expected to spend his wedding night—or it wouldn't have been if he'd ever considered getting married before now.

But the odd hollowness in his gut had begun the instant she'd dismissed the earth-moving kiss as *no big deal*. When he'd pulled her into his arms, he'd expected the urgent need to get her clothes off and have his way with her. It was the other sensation he'd experienced, the one not tied to anything corporeal, that would require privacy and time to sort out.

"I'm your business partner," she retorted, snatching her hand back.

Damn. She was beautiful with her brown eyes shooting sparks and outrage painting her high cheekbones with rosy patches. As quickly as it had flared, his temper dissipated. She wasn't someone he could afford to alienate even if it would make keeping his distance that much easier.

"And you're doing me a huge favor." He inclined his head. "I'm starting to understand why you took sex off the table. Things between us are a little too volatile, aren't they?"

Violet nodded in obvious relief. "I think we will be fine as long as we stick to the plan."

"A plan we can start to flesh out after a good night's sleep."

"I'll see you in the morning."

JT walked out the door and heard the click of the latch behind him. He strode down the hall to the master bedroom and without turning on a light, crossed the room to the double French doors that led out onto the terrace. Throwing them open, he stepped into the night. His nerves were a tangle, too raw to allow him to enjoy the desert air or the crescent moon that hung low in the clear sky.

Did Violet have any idea how close she'd come to being ravished tonight? First she'd shown up for their wedding in that romantic lace dress. Then she'd flirted with him over a glass of champagne. The final straw was complaining that he hadn't given her a proper kiss at their wedding. Was she trying to drive him mad or did she honestly not have a clue what she did to him?

It was the latter, JT suspected, gripping the terrace railing hard. And where she was concerned, he was his own worst enemy. When she'd stared at him with her big soulful eyes all soft and earnest, the consequent firing of all his nerve endings had short-circuited his self-preservation.

So now what was he supposed to do with all this pent-up hunger for her?

It had been one thing when he sat in her bar night after night, driving himself crazy with lurid fantasies he'd never act on. He could enjoy tangling with her verbally, knowing that her open, sunny nature would eventually grow tired of his talent for closing himself off. She'd said it herself. She knew nothing about him. He hadn't let her in. He never let anyone in.

And yet, she knew things about his past few others did. His uncle had told her about his mother's addiction so Violet had some idea how miserable his childhood had been. She would want to talk about all the things that had happened when he was young. He would resent her questions. Withdraw even further. When it came to intimacy and love, he lacked the skills to find happiness.

She wouldn't want to be with him until she'd solved all his problems. Made him see the silver lining in everything that had happened in his past. She'd expect him to come around to her positive way of thinking and would grow frustrated when he didn't.

A splash from the pool below drew his attention. Violet swam through the turquoise water, her stroke powerful and elegant. JT watched her as she came up for air at the far end of the pool. Once again she dove under. She used her feet and legs to push away from the wall with great power. When she surfaced, she headed for the opposite wall in a strong freestyle.

He watched her lap the pool for fifteen minutes. Her focus and determination amazed him. It was how she approached everything, he decided. Once she set her mind to something, she wasn't going to be deterred.

At long last her energy seemed to burn itself out. She lazed in the middle of the pool and her stillness roused JT to the uncomfortable realization that she was naked. Cursing, he pushed away from the railing and headed for the stairs that led down from his terrace to the pool house and lounge area.

He enjoyed throwing parties and often his guests forgot to bring a suit along so he kept a stock of bathing suits in the pool house for their use. By the time he found a bikini he thought might fit Violet, she had gotten out of the pool and had wrapped herself in a towel. She looked up in surprise as he approached.

"Next time you decide to go swimming," he began, holding up the bikini he'd selected, "I'd appreciate it if you didn't skinny-dip."

"I'm sorry," she murmured, taking the bathing suit from him. Water streamed from her long dark hair, dampening the towel. "I didn't realize you'd still be up."

It eased his irritation a little that she looked so utterly mortified to have been caught. "Like you, I'm often still working at this hour."

"Thanks for the suit. I won't bother you any further tonight."

Was she kidding? He'd never get to sleep with the tantalizing glimpses he'd had of her naked body parading through his thoughts. JT ground his teeth as she retreated toward the house. Only when her towel-clad form had disappeared from view did he return to the master suite.

At least one positive thing about this marriage in name only was that they didn't have to live under the same roof. After less than an hour alone in his house with her, he was a finger snap away from tossing her over his shoulder and spiriting her off to his bed.

Thank goodness he wasn't going to share his living space with her day and night. His control would snap like a dry twig if he had to put up with her sassy humor and artless sensuality. Before she could remind him of their agreement, he'd have her in his bed, her beautiful body writhing in pleasure.

Making love to her would only be the beginning. Soon she'd be ferreting out all his ugly childhood secrets and he'd be living in fear that something she discovered would be so awful she'd cut him out of her life.

And then he'd be alone again, turned inside out, his raw emotions exposed for all the world to see. No. That was something that could never happen. And if he kept her at arms' length, it wouldn't.

Four

At eight the next morning, Violet found JT in the room he'd dubbed his playroom. She paused just outside the door, needing a second to collect her wits before approaching him.

Clad in worn jeans and a black cotton button-down shirt, he was bent over what looked to be an antique pool table. With his left hand, he rolled the eight ball toward the far bumper and caught it as it returned, all the while studying the papers scattered over the table's beige felt. The briefcase she'd filled with Tiberius's files sat empty on the floor beside his bare feet.

Being confronted by so much casual masculinity first thing in the morning wasn't fair. Especially not after she'd lain awake staring at the ceiling until the sun starting lightening the horizon, regretting that she'd kissed him, wishing she'd dropped her towel when he confronted her on the pool deck. Her conflicting desires were tearing her apart. She'd have to choose one path and commit to it.

"Did you get some tea?" he asked without glancing her way.

His question made her realize she'd been silently staring at him for far too long. "Your housekeeper made me a cup. It's delicious." She didn't need to ask why his kitchen was stocked with four different blends of green tea. She already suspected the house saw a lot of guests. While in Miami, JT had been known for his parties. She doubted much had changed in the last six years. "Find anything that might help us?"

"My uncle accumulated copious amounts of information and enjoyed making detailed notes on all his business dealings. Every share he bought is documented. What I'm missing is the information on the family members who turned him down."

She drew close enough to the table to see that he'd created two lists of names. From past experience she knew how much Tiberius loved to collect information. The files from his home office overflowed with details—some of them helpful, most of them too trivial to waste time on.

"Let me help. Maybe I can speed things up."

She waited for him to acknowledge her offer, but he remained lost in thought. Had he not heard her, or did he want to handle everything himself? If it was the latter, too bad. She'd come up with this plan and intended to be involved at every stage. Running her gaze down JT's list of relatives who still owned their stock, she saw he'd notated which ones were definitely in Preston's pocket.

"You should know Paul and Tiberius had a huge argument three years ago," she said, indicating his mother's cousin. "Something about a rare comic book that Tiberius and Paul supposedly bought together using Tiberius's money when they were eight. Paul kept the comic book, but never paid Tiberius for his half and now it's worth like ten grand."

She shook her head. No matter what the comic's worth, it was silly to still be feuding about it all these years later, but Tiberius wasn't one to forgive a slight. She glanced at JT's strong profile. It was a characteristic Tiberius shared with his nephew.

"Thanks." JT made a note next to Paul's name and returned to the file he'd been reading.

"You've gotten a lot done." She assessed how he'd organized the files, and then pulled five out to make a third pile. As she finished, she noticed JT's glare. "What?"

"I had a system."

"And now it's better." She flipped open the top file and pointed to a gossip article about his third cousin. "Casey is in the middle of a nasty divorce. He has a mistress with very expensive taste tucked away and I believe she sees herself as the next Mrs. Casey Stone. Then there's the problems he's been having with his investment firm. He'd probably be receptive to an influx of cash."

JT looked no less displeased. "My father has done several favors for Casey. He has no interest in selling his stock to me, nor would he throw his votes in my direction."

Violet opened her mouth to argue, but decided from JT's set expression that she'd be wasting her breath. Instead, she set Casey's folder aside and opened the next one. She sifted through several documents before arriving at the one she wanted. "Your great aunt Harriet has recently come under the influence of a rather clever con man who has convinced her to fund his charity in New Orleans." Seeing the flicker of interest in JT's gaze, she sidled closer. "I can be a big help. No one knew the way Tiberius's mind worked better than me. Did you know that over the past thirty years Tiberius had collected a storage unit full of Las Vegas history? Some of it was significant. Most of it was trivial nonsense. He left the entire collection to Scarlett for her *Mob Experience* exhibit."

"I'm sure that's fascinating, but you've done enough." He pushed away from the pool table and nodded toward the open door. "Have Pauline fix you some breakfast. I'll take you back to Fontaine Chic when you're finished."

She repressed a protest. Assuming he'd accept her as his business partner just because she'd come up with the idea of getting married was shortsighted. A man as closed off as JT wasn't going to jump at the chance to work with her. If she didn't accept that, frustration was going to make her crazy.

"Before we head back to town, there are a few things we should talk about."

"Such as?" He crossed his arms over his chest.

"How would you like me to explain this?" She held up her left hand and indicated the ring with her right pointer finger.

For a moment he didn't speak, just stared at the ring. "However you'd like."

Violet gnashed her teeth and tried a different approach. "What are you planning to say about our impulsive wedding last night?"

"If it comes up, I will say we've been involved for almost a year, but we've been keeping it quiet."

"And that's it?"

"I do not expect anyone will press me for details."

"Truly?" How could he not comprehend people's curiosity? "You don't think someone will ask where we met? How long we've been seeing each other?"

"They won't."

"Isn't there anyone in your life you share things with?"

His isolation continued to baffle her. Did he choose to keep everyone out of his life or was he such a pain in the ass that no one was interested?

"My staff knows better than to show an interest in my personal life and those I see socially aren't interested in my business dealings. Since our arrangement falls in neither of those categories, I won't have to explain our marriage to anyone."

"That's great for you," she retorted sarcastically. "But I have two sisters and a mother, who when they hear I got married, are going to expect me to share every juicy detail of what we're doing and why."

At last he gave her his full attention. "There are no juicy details."

She shoved her hands into the back pocket of her jeans to keep from acting on the desire to jolt him out of his stoic calm. "Can I tell them what we're really doing?"

"Do you trust them to keep the truth to themselves?"

Given his tendency to play his cards close to the vest, the question shouldn't have shocked her as much as it did. "I trust them completely."

She bared her teeth in a spiteful grin. "But if you don't think I should, I could tell them that you've pined over me for years, but were too afraid that Tiberius would ruin you if you made your feelings known."

Irritation tightened his mouth into a thin line. "They won't believe something so ridiculous."

"Scarlett will." Violet gave free rein to the demon riding her shoulder. Being reasonable hadn't worked, and she badly wanted a peek at the hand he held. Time to play dirty. Maybe if she antagonized him, he'd let something slip. "She already has it in her head that you show up in Baccarat every night because you want me."

If he denied it, she wouldn't be surprised.

"And she bases that on what exactly?" His even tone gave nothing away.

Violet found herself in deeper water than she expected. Nothing for her to do but swim hard for shore and hope she wasn't eaten by sharks. "The way you look at me."

"And how exactly do I look at you?"

Violet frowned, trying to remember exactly how her sister had phrased it. "She said you look hungry."

JT might be a master at hiding his thoughts, but Violet swore she saw a slight widening of his eyes. To her delight, she'd scored if not a direct hit, then one fairly close to the mark. Fascinating. She was pondering the possibility that he wasn't as disinterested in her as he'd claimed when he spoke up.

"Your sister has a flare for the drama," he said. "She's fallen in love and sees nothing but potential love matches all around her."

"You're probably right."

But he hadn't actually come out and denied it. Violet decided she'd pushed enough for one day. Much more and she'd run the risk that he'd become even more enigmatic. By allowing herself this tiny win, she now had something she could build on. It was like gaining the trust of a wild creature. Better to use short positive sessions to get them to drop their guard than to try and rush things and make it more skittish.

"Have you eaten?" she asked.

"An hour ago."

She masked her disappointment. "I'll eat something quick and be ready to go back to town in half an hour if that works for you."

"I think I'm in a place where I can take a break and I could use another cup of coffee." He scooped an empty mug off the edge of the pool table and followed her out of his playroom.

Violet's pulse kicked into high gear. Maybe she'd learned the secret to dealing with JT: she'd pretend she didn't care if he spent time with her or included her in his plans to take over his family business and wait for him to come to her. It wasn't the way she was accustomed to dealing with the men she got involved with. Most of the time they liked her to take the lead.

That would never be the case with JT.

"You were right about the view," she remarked a half hour later. She and JT were sitting in the breakfast nook just off the kitchen. The wall-to-wall windows offered a panoramic view of the desert and the mountains to the north that speared an impossibly blue sky. "Do you miss the ocean? Growing up in Miami, I would think the desert would be hard to get used to."

"At first I was worried that I'd hate the dust and the heat, but the mountains make it all worthwhile. And if I need to get on the water, I have a boat on Lake Mead."

Something about the view or sharing a meal—he'd sampled her eggs and stolen half the fruit off her plate—had worked some sort of magic on him. For the last half hour he'd been almost…charming. And Violet was loath to break the spell. So she sipped tea and nibbled on toast, delaying the end of the meal so she could prolong her time with this more accessible version of her new husband.

"Sounds like the best of both worlds." She popped a grape into her mouth. "I am curious though, why are you living on a horse ranch out here instead of closer to Titanium?"

"My grandmother grew up on a horse farm in Kentucky." He took Violet's left hand and regarded the ring he'd put on her hand to seal his wedding vows. "Even after she married my grandfather and moved to Miami, she kept several show jumpers. Starting when I was five, my mother used to take me to watch her. I'd sit in the stands and marvel at how she and her horse flew over six-foot-high jumps."

As he spoke, his gaze grew less focused. He'd stopped seeing his grandmother's ring and was revisiting a happy moment from his past. The muscles of his face relaxed into a fond half smile. Violet watched him with dawning wonder. This wasn't the first time he'd opened up to her—after all, he'd shared his decision to quit his family's company. But it was the first time he'd shared a happy memory from his childhood.

Based on their interaction to this point, she'd labeled him as guarded and brooding. She'd assumed his unhappy childhood had left him emotionally shut down and incapable of letting joy in. But maybe it wasn't that he didn't feel but that he felt too much? If he was a powder keg ready to explode, what happened when someone lit a match?

"She insisted I learn to ride," JT continued, oblivious to the thoughts churning inside Violet's head. "During the summer, she would take me to her family's horse farm in Kentucky and we would spend hours riding. When I was good enough to compete, she took me to horse shows. It all stopped when she died."

JT had lost his grandmother when he was ten. Hearing him speak so warmly of her, Violet suspected he'd been devastated to lose the one person who'd showered him with love and attention. She remembered what a tough time Tiberius had gone through when his mother had died. He'd taken Lucille and Violet to the funeral and she remembered how unwelcome they'd been.

"I never had any grandparents around when I was a kid," she told him. "My mom left Cincinnati when she was seventeen and never looked back." She smiled wryly. "And you know the situation on my father's side."

"I've never met any of my father's relatives. His parents died when he was very young."

"I remember Tiberius saying something about that. I guess I didn't realize Preston didn't keep in touch with his family. Wasn't he from California? Have you ever thought about looking some of them up?"

The shutters were back over JT's eyes. As soon as he'd

mentioned his father, his expression became as remote as the mountaintops that made his view so extraordinary.

"No."

His abrupt answer discouraged further conversation on that topic. Violet sighed as she realized JT was done sharing.

"If you don't mind," she began, setting her napkin on the table beside her plate. "I think it's time I headed back to Fontaine Chic."

"I'll get my keys."

While JT waited in the foyer for Violet to collect her overnight bag, he replayed their conversation in his mind and revisited every expression on her lovely face. He'd enjoyed sharing breakfast with her. So much so that instead of giving her a brief, dry explanation of why he'd chosen ranch life over a house in the city, he'd gone all sentimental on her and let her see how his grandmother had influenced him.

Nor did it surprise him how tempted he was to trust her. Her earnest curiosity and upbeat outlook weren't a clever cover for ulterior motives. She honestly wanted to help. Her impulsive suggestion that they get married so he could get control of Tiberius's Stone Properties stock had demonstrated she was far too quick to believe in people.

Take him for example. She expected him to stick to their understanding that this wasn't a real marriage. Which meant hands off. And the best—no, only—way he could think of to honor their agreement was to stay as far away from her as possible.

"Ready when you are," she said, as descended the stairs. She was a feminine marvel in a pastel floral dress with thin straps that bared her delicate shoulders and a full skirt that flirted with her knees. Pink sandals with three-inch heels drew attention to her spectacular calves and her hair was swept up into a loose top-knot. She made his mouth water.

With a slight bounce, she stepped from the stairs onto the foyer's marble floor and crossed to where he stood by the front door, tongue-tied, his hormones in an uproar. As she neared, he snagged her luggage and opened the door.

"I don't think we should live together," he stated, his voice short and clipped.

"How are people going to believe we are married if we don't?"

"We both work a lot. No one will notice."

Her lips thinned. "That's not going to work."

"We'll talk about it when I return to town."

She eyed the second overnight bag he held. "Where are you going?"

"As soon as I drop you off, I'm heading to North Carolina." The sooner he secured the necessary shares of Stone Properties, the sooner he could replace his father as CEO. And the sooner he could be free of this marriage-in-name-only before he did something to change their relationship forever.

"Who's there?"

"My cousin Brent. His dad's Alzheimer's has made it necessary for him to take charge of the finances in the last few months. He has several thousand shares. It's not all that I need, but every bit helps."

"I don't recall seeing him in Tiberius's files."

JT held the passenger door open and gritted his teeth against the sweet seduction of her perfume as she brushed past him and slid into the car. Damn, but she was a tempting armful. Resisting the impulse to reprise last night's kiss actually caused a dull ache in his gut. When he'd agreed to marry her, he'd underestimated just how challenging it would be to keep his hands to himself.

"He's not." After depositing their bags in the trunk, JT

got behind the wheel and started the BMW. "I don't know why Tiberius didn't include him."

The car picked up speed as he drove down his long driveway toward the highway and JT noticed that the air-flow in the open convertible whipped Violet's skirt into a frenzy of dancing flowers and bared a whole lot of lean, toned thigh. He daydreamed about sliding his hands along the soft, smooth length of her leg and finding her hot and wet and eager for him. It wasn't until a truck flashed past on a perpendicular course that he realized they'd reached the end of his driveway. JT slammed on his brakes and the BMW skidded to a halt.

"Are you okay?" he asked, glancing her way.

She regarded him curiously. "I'm fine. Are you?"

Not even close. "I think we'll be more comfortable with the top up." He hit the button that raised the convertible top and while it was closing, stared at his grandfather's ring on his left hand.

Yeah, staying as far from her as possible for the next couple months was the only way he was going to survive this marriage with his heart intact.

On the thirty-minute ride to Las Vegas, he kept his eyes to himself and his thoughts on the trip ahead. Violet seemed to understand his need to plan because she kept her gaze on the passing landscape, only occasionally glancing down at her ever-vibrating smartphone.

Finally, JT had to ask, "Is it always this way for you?"

"I'm sorry?" She blinked as if she had a hard time re-focusing her attention on him.

"Your phone. It's been going off non-stop since we got in the car."

A wry smile curved her lips. "It's my sisters. I'm not usually off the grid for twelve hours."

Envy stabbed at JT. What would it be like to have someone fret about your wellbeing? Nice? Smothering? "They must be worried about you. Why don't you answer them?"

"I sent them a text last night. They know I'm safe." Her smile developed sharp edges. "I told them I was with you."

JT ignored the way his pulse leapt at the challenge in her manner. She would take any opening he gave her to provoke him; what she didn't realize was that once unleashed, his emotions would overwhelm them both.

"Did you explain that we got married?"

"I didn't want to do that in a text."

"Then what do they think you are doing with me?" His body tensed, but the sensation was pleasurable rather than distressing.

"Probably what most of the women do when they spend the night at your house."

Damn her sass. "Why would you want your sisters to think we slept together?"

She didn't answer him immediately, and when she did speak, all amusement had fled her voice. "I suppose that's something else we should discuss."

"Aren't we already discussing it?" Her change of topic made him feel as if he was spinning in place.

"Do you intend to bring women home while we're married?"

Her question sparked a ridiculous urge to snatch her into his arms and kiss her silly. He wasn't allowed to make love to her, but she didn't want him having sex with anyone else? "I hadn't really thought about it."

"I know our marriage isn't real, but I'd appreciate it if you could refrain from dating other women until we can get divorced."

"I think I can last a couple months."

"What if you can't get the shares or the votes you need in time for the annual stockholders' meeting?"

"What are you asking?"

"Our goal was to make you CEO," she said, her manner matter-of-fact. "If that doesn't happen in the next few months it's because we didn't have enough time. You aren't horrible to be married to. I could see sticking it out for another year."

A year of being married to Violet with the temptation of making love to her eating him alive? JT recoiled from the thought. "We'll get divorced in the fall regardless."

Her expression was inscrutable as she nodded. "Then we'll get divorced."

Conversation dried up after their exchange. Fortunately they'd reached the city limits and traffic wasn't as backed up as usual, so their journey to her hotel was accomplished quickly. He swung the BMW into Fontaine Chic's circular driveway and stopped the car by the lobby doors. Before he could shut off the car, Violet put a hand on his arm.

"If you just open the trunk, I'll grab my bag."

In that instant, JT realized the last thing he wanted to do was fly off and leave his brand-new wife to her own devices. What an idiotic notion. They weren't really married. It wasn't as if they'd shared a grand night of passion he couldn't wait to duplicate. But she was already far more important to him than a casual acquaintance, which—their connection to Tiberius aside—was all they were.

"I'll call you and let you know how things went in North Carolina." He slipped the garage remote off the visor and extended it to her. "Here."

Her brows came together briefly. "Why would you give me that?"

Because he liked the idea of her sleeping—and skinny-dipping—in his home.

"Our house," he corrected her. "I might need some information from Tiberius's files. It would be useful if you could get to them."

"Let me get this straight." A playful light glinted in her eyes. "You're going to let me help and you're going to trust me alone in *our* house?"

"Are you planning on digging through my underwear drawer?"

She leaned close and whispered, "Is that where you keep your secrets?"

No, those were all locked up in his head. "Please feel free to investigate and see."

"It doesn't bother you to have me snooping?"

To his surprise, it didn't. "What do you think you'll find?"

"I don't know." She plucked the opener from his grasp. "But everything about you is such a closed book I'm sure I'll find the most mundane of things utterly fascinating."

With a sassy wink she slipped from the car and collected her bag. JT watched until she'd sashayed through the lobby door before shifting into drive. He'd been married to her for less than twenty-four hours and already he was noticing cracks in his defenses. Sunshine was seeping in, illuminating emotions that hadn't seen the light of day in over eighteen years. He felt lighter, more optimistic as if her positive outlook was contagious.

It took all his determination to put aside thoughts of his new wife and her unsettling effect on him, but by the time JT reached long-term parking, he'd managed to focus his attention on the trip ahead. Earlier that morning he'd had his assistant book a flight from Vegas to Charlotte. He'd decided to fly commercial instead of borrowing the company jet. He didn't want his father to start questioning why he was traveling all over the East Coast.

After parking his car, he headed to the terminal. An email message arrived on his phone as he exited security. His secretary had forwarded his itinerary for the coming week. He was booked from Charlotte to Atlanta to Louisville and finally up to New York City. Four cities in six days. He hoped like hell it would be a profitable trip.

Five

As soon as Violet entered Fontaine Chic, she headed straight for her office. Since no one had called her in a panic, she assumed nothing earthshaking had happened in the last twelve hours, but she wanted to touch base with her assistant. Patty brought Violet a cup of tea and the previous day's report. Violet crossed to the seating area near the window and sat down on the couch. A quick scan assured Violet that her hotel continued to run smoothly in her absence. Now to address the problem of convincing her sisters that marrying JT didn't mean she'd lost her marbles.

I'm back.

She sent the text to both Scarlett and Harper and wasn't surprised how fast the responses came.

I'm on my way. From Scarlett.

Give me twenty minutes and don't tell Scarlett a thing until I get there. From Harper.

With a fatalistic sigh, Violet set the phone down on the coffee table. Exhaustion washed over her as her night of little sleep caught up to her. She let her muscles relax. Her head fell back against the comfortable leather couch. Almost immediately she was besieged by hysterical amusement. Had she seriously just married JT? Demanded that he give her a proper kiss? Not that there was anything proper in the way his tongue had coasted against hers. She shivered as the memory swept over her.

"I demand to hear every last detail immediately," Scarlett proclaimed from the doorway.

Violet's eyes flew open. She hadn't even realized she'd closed them. "Harper said to wait."

"You don't seriously think I'm going to sit here in suspense for twenty minutes, do you?" Scarlett flopped onto the couch beside Violet and pinned her with a steely glare. "Spill."

Now that the moment had arrived, Violet decided it was harder to justify her actions than she'd imagined. "I really think we should wait. I don't want to explain myself twice."

She wasn't sure she wanted to explain herself *once*.

Scarlett waved Violet's objection away. "What's there to explain? You finally gave in to the chemistry between you and JT. Was it fabulous? Is he an intense lover? He has such great hands and those lips…"

Violet choked back a laugh. "Scarlett!"

"What? Harper will want to lecture you on moving too fast. I won't get to hear any of the hot stuff once she shows up."

"There is no hot stuff."

"Really?" Scarlett's face reflected disappointment. "I would have thought there'd be major fireworks between you."

"It wasn't like that."

"Then why are you blushing?"

Violet put her hands to her cheeks and found them on fire. "He caught me skinny-dipping in his pool."

"And…?" Scarlett leaned forward, her eyes wide and encouraging.

"He handed me a bikini and told me to wear it next time I wanted to take a swim."

Scarlett sat back and regarded her sister in absolute confusion. Violet had never seen her so utterly baffled.

"I thought your text said you spent the night with JT."

"I did. Only not the way your naughty mind thinks. I slept at his house."

Before Scarlett could reply, Harper breezed into the room. She was slightly out of breath as she demanded, "What did I miss?"

"Not a darned thing," Scarlett muttered in disgust. "Apparently there's nothing for her to tell."

"What about that?" Harper settled next to Scarlett and reached across her to point at Violet's left hand.

Scarlett snatched up the hand and stared at the ring. "You're engaged?"

"Not exactly," Violet murmured.

"That looks like an engagement ring."

"Actually it's a wedding ring. JT and I got married last night at the Tunnel of Love Chapel."

"Married?" Scarlett gaped at her sister.

"JT Stone?" Harper shook her head. "Have you told Grandfather? Are you at all worried how he'll react when he finds out you're married to the competition?"

"I'm going to call him in a little while." Violet was all prepared with a rational explanation for her actions. "He'll understand when I explain what happened."

"What did happen?" Scarlett asked. "The last time I mentioned him being interested in you, I got the distinct impression you had no intention of letting anything develop."

"It hasn't exactly developed the way you think," Violet said.

"You're married," Harper pointed out. "Something had to happen between you."

"It's all a little complicated."

"Did Rick slip something special into one of his signature cocktails?" Scarlett narrowed her eyes. "By that I mean, were you drunk?"

"I was perfectly sober." Violet rushed to answer the question in Harper's eyes. "So was he."

"So, you didn't just spend the night at JT's house," Harper clarified. "You spent the night with JT?"

"No. It's not that kind of marriage."

Harper regarded her gravely. "What sort of marriage is it?"

"It's strictly a business arrangement."

"But not funny business obviously," Scarlett groused.

Violet ignored her. "Mom and I went to the lawyer a few days ago and it turns out Tiberius had been purchasing Stone Properties stock from other family members."

"I thought he didn't want anything to do with the company after what Preston did to him," Scarlett said.

"I think it was more a matter of not being able to do anything to get his brother-in-law removed as CEO. Preston controlled the shares he inherited on his wife's death as well as the ones that were in JT's trust. Shares that JT took control of on his thirtieth birthday two months ago."

"How much stock had Tiberius managed to buy?" Harper asked, her keen business mind catching on quickly.

"Eighteen percent."

"And how much was in JT's trust?"

"Thirty percent. Preston owns thirty and the other twenty-two percent is split up among the family."

"So what does this have to do with why you and JT got married?" Scarlett asked, returning the conversation to what she was interested in.

"Obviously Tiberius left her his shares," Harper said.

Scarlett shot her sister a pained look. "I get that, but why marry JT when she could sell him the shares?"

"Because according to Tiberius's will, I have to keep the stock until Preston dies."

"You know you didn't have to marry JT," Harper pointed out. "You could have just thrown your support behind him."

Violet felt her features take on the same injured expression Scarlett had just worn. Once in a while she wished Harper would acknowledge that she wasn't always the smartest one in the room.

"Only family can vote the shares," she explained.

Scarlett clapped her hands in delight. "So, now you're family. That's brilliant."

"Thank you." Violet appreciated having Scarlett's support because she could see that Harper wasn't done with her objections.

"But with your eighteen percent and JT's thirty—"

Violet interrupted. "We still need three percent to control the vote." She glanced at the clock on her phone and realized JT was probably boarding his flight to Charlotte. "He's heading out to talk to some of his relatives, hoping he can persuade enough of them to either sell or throw their vote his way so he can take control of Stone Properties and get his father out."

"And you found out about this a few days ago?" Harper frowned. "Aren't you moving a little quick? I would think you'd both want to protect yourselves before getting married."

"You haven't seen the way JT looks at her," Scarlett interjected. "I don't think that man has the patience to last any longer."

To Violet's intense dismay, she felt her cheeks heating again. "It's not like that between us," she protested. "And we signed an agreement that we'd walk away with what we came into the marriage with. Really, it's just a business deal. A marriage in name only."

"How long do think that's going to last?" Scarlett's lips wore a lusty smile. "The two of you share the same house night after night. Him just down the hall? I give you a week tops before you crack. JT…" She cocked her head and considered. "Maybe three days."

"We're not going to live together," Violet explained, growing lightheaded as she remembered how hard it had been to fall asleep the previous night after kissing JT. But in the future there would be no more such kisses, passion-drenched or otherwise. They'd both agreed on that.

"You're not?" Scarlett looked scandalized at the thought.

"Lots of married couple don't," Harper said. "My parents being one of them."

And their marital separation was what had led to Ross's numerous affairs and the two daughters he'd never acknowledged. Or maybe his affairs had led to his estrangement from his wife. Violet had never asked Harper what she thought. As close as the three girls had become in the last five years, some topics remained uncomfortable.

"Are you sure you know what you're doing?" Harper continued. "I mean, how well do you know JT?"

"Not as well as she's going to get to know him," Scarlett put in slyly.

Violet shot her a repressive look. "I don't know how to explain it, but he feels like family. I know until recently that Tiberius refused to have anything to do with him, but he talked so much about his sister and what life was like for JT as a kid, I feel as if I know him." She regarded each of her sisters, trying to gauge if she was making sense.

"I get how sometimes you can feel as if you know a person even though you've never met," Harper said, a note of tension in her voice. "But often the reality is very different and you have to be careful."

Was Harper referring to JT or her own problems with celebrity chef Ashton Croft, whose latest restaurant was

supposed to have opened in Harper's Fontaine Ciel hotel
two weeks earlier? The charismatic executive chef-turned-
television sensation was unconventional and passionate
about food and adventure. Since starting negotiations with
Harper for the restaurant, he'd been a thorn in her side with
one outrageous demand after another.

Violet suspected her sister had been a Chef Ashton fan
long before the restaurant deal. Harper's DVR was filled
with Croft's television series, *The Culinary Wanderer*, in
which he traveled around the world in search of the perfect meal. Why such an adventurous wanderer appealed
to someone as methodical and strategic as Harper, Violet
would never understand.

"I'll admit that what I know of JT is already proving
incomplete." Violet considered what she'd learned over
breakfast. He'd opened up to give her a glimpse into his
past. A happy moment in what she suspected was a turbulent childhood. "But I don't think he has any intention
of cheating me." And any heartbreak that happened would
be because she'd let it.

Harper shook her head. "I just hope you know what
you're doing."

"So do I," Violet muttered. "So do I."

JT should have known that letting Violet's optimism
rub off on him was reckless, but he'd been seduced by
her earnest smiles and luminous brown eyes. Now, with
a tumbler of excellent scotch on his knee, he allowed his
gaze to drift around his cousin's mahogany-paneled study
and tried not to let his disappointment show.

"Sorry, JT." Brent looked as if the weight of the world
rested on his shoulders. "My dad sold the shares to Preston five months ago. You're welcome to the hundred I received on my eighteenth birthday."

"Thanks for the offer, but I'd rather you remain a stockholder and help me convince the rest of the family that my dad's management isn't doing the company any favors." No wonder Tiberius hadn't created a file on Brent's father. What was the point when the shares were already lost? "Any idea why your father sold the shares to my dad? It's not as if the two of them got along."

Brent snorted. "That's an understatement. My dad hated yours. He blamed Preston for your mom's death."

Brent's father Ted was Tiberius and Fiona's first cousin. He'd been as close to them as a sibling, but Ted and Fiona's relationship had grown a bit strained over what had happened to Tiberius When Brent's dad had told Fiona her husband was out of control, she'd resolutely defended her husband. Preston became a sore spot between them, but their love remained as strong as ever.

"Then why did he sell him the shares?"

"After it happened, he felt horrible. Preston convinced him that your mom wanted more shares for you."

"Your father didn't remember that my mom's been dead for eighteen years?"

Brent grimaced. "I knew then I had to get power of attorney and take over his finances."

"He's getting worse faster than you expected, isn't he?"

"His lucid moments are fewer and fewer." Father and son had enjoyed a close connection that JT had long envied.

"Sorry," JT said. "I can't imagine how hard this is for you."

"Most people can't." Ted had been an intelligent, intuitive businessman. It had to be tearing Brent apart to lose his father this way. To watch him slip away a little more each day, knowing there was no way to ever get him back. "It's tough watching a clever, bold businessman like my father forget the dog's name or where the kitchen is in the house."

The deep throb in Brent's voice made JT's chest hurt. "Is there anything you need? Anything I can help with?" He regretted that in his preoccupation with his own troubles, he'd not kept up with his cousin the way a friend should.

Brent cleared his throat. "That's the worst of it. There's nothing anyone can do." He swallowed the last of his scotch. "But I appreciate the offer. You're not just family, you're a good friend."

A year apart in age, they'd spent time together as kids, forming bonds that made them close as adults. Fiona Stone had often traveled to Charlotte to visit her favorite cousin. JT remembered how, in this Neoclassical-style house, built more than a hundred years ago, his mother hadn't needed drugs or alcohol to cope with her life. She'd smiled all the time and given him big hugs and spoiled him with ice cream sundaes and trips to the zoo and museums. Getting his mother back had been like a miracle. But neither the trip nor his mother's happiness could last forever.

"So, why don't you tell me what's going on. Why you're suddenly buying up stock."

"I want to get control of Stone Properties."

"Seriously?" Curiosity flared in Brent's gray eyes. "And how are you planning to do that?"

"For the last six months, Tiberius had been quietly buying shares."

"That clever son of a bitch," Brent exclaimed in admiration. "So, you two were going to team up?"

JT shook his head. "I had no idea what he was planning. You know Tiberius."

"Kept his cards close to his chest. And who could blame him after what your dad did to him. How much of the company had he managed to get?"

"Eighteen percent."

"And with the thirty you came into on your last birthday, you are three percent short of control."

"It's a little more complicated than that," JT explained, thinking of Violet and her damned skinny-dipping. "Turns out, Tiberius didn't leave me the shares."

"Really?" Brent got up to refresh their drink.

"Thanks to my dad, my uncle and I weren't on the best of terms, but in the last month or so we'd started to reconnect." JT considered all the tales his father had told him about Tiberius and wished he'd been smarter about where he'd put his loyalty.

Brent frowned. "So who owns his shares?"

"Tiberius's unofficially adopted daughter." JT held up his left hand and showed off his grandfather's ring. "Last night we got married."

The number of times JT had successfully surprised his quick-witted cousin could be counted on one hand. Today marked the fifth one.

"You're married to...oh, what's her name?" Brent snapped his fingers as he searched his memory.

"Violet Fontaine."

"Tiberius took in her and her mother, didn't he?" Uncertainty fogged Brent's gaze. "But I thought her last name was Allen?"

"Turns out she's Ross Fontaine's illegitimate daughter. After he died, Violet's grandfather—Henry Fontaine, head of Fontaine Resorts and Hotels—came to Vegas to find her and make amends for his son's neglect. She's in line to succeed the old man as head of the company."

"And you married her instead of buying the stock?" Brent asked, sounding very much as if he thought JT wasn't thinking clearly. "If you're short on cash, you could have come to me."

A year ago Brent had sold the company he'd started

and had not yet found a place to invest the four billion he'd made.

"The terms of Tiberius's will don't allow her to part with the stock in any way until my dad dies."

"Good old Tiberius." Brent grinned in admiration. "And until you married her, she couldn't vote because she's not family."

JT knew he could count on his cousin to grasp the entire problem. "That sums it up."

Brent blew out a worried breath. "When your dad finds out about this, things are going to get nasty."

"That's why I need to meet with as much family as I can before he finds out."

With regret tugging his dark eyebrows together, Brent said, "I wish I could help you out."

"Me, too."

His cousin was one hell of a businessman. His father had taught him well. Again JT felt the twinge of envy. Why did bad things happen to good people while manipulative bastards like JT's father sailed through life unscathed?

"Where are you off to next?" Brent asked.

"Atlanta."

"Cousin Skip." JT's cousin rolled his eyes. "I don't envy you."

Six

At midnight, Baccarat's couches and barstools were occupied by a twenty-something clientele with palates sophisticated enough for Rick's special blends. As Violet crossed the threshold into the lounge, her pulse escalated but she immediately told herself to calm down. Even if JT was in town, it was too late for him to be at the bar. She usually swung through here at eleven-fifteen, but tonight she'd been held up by the manager of the sports book.

The only contact she'd had with JT in the last several days was a series of terse text messages, each less hopeful than the last. He was having no luck finding more shares to buy. His father had either bought up what he could or had convinced his family to vote with him.

Her phone vibrated, indicating a text message had come in. Someone at the front desk was looking for her. Violet left Baccarat without catching Rick's attention and headed for the lobby.

As she approached, she saw a tall man standing with the night manager. The stranger had his back to her, but when Violet was five feet away, he turned his head and she glimpsed his profile.

She almost stopped dead in her tracks. Preston Rhodes? What the hell was he doing here?

JT's father hadn't spotted her yet, but she was too exposed to make a run for it without drawing unwanted attention. Gathering a deep breath, Violet stiffened her spine and marched forward.

"Good evening," she said, doubting her ability to pretend she had no idea who Preston was. Although the man had never appeared in Vegas before, she recognized him from articles she'd read about him. And then there was the resemblance to JT around the man's eyes and chin. "Preston Rhodes, isn't it?"

While the night manager returned to his post, Violet held out her hand and wasn't surprised when Preston clasped it in a punishing handshake. Of course the man would choose to demonstrate his power with brute force. That he wouldn't pull any punches just because she was a woman wasn't as flattering as it might have been if he were someone else.

"Ms. Fontaine." His smooth tone did little to hide the poisonous nature of the man's character. "Or should I call you Violet since we're now family?"

She tried to keep her surprise from showing. His thin laugh let her know that she hadn't been successful. JT hadn't mentioned that he'd told his father. Irritation flared. She wished he'd warned her. Facing someone like Preston without preparation was better suited to Harper, who had a knack for staying calm no matter what the catastrophe.

"Mr. Rhodes—"

"Preston," he corrected, a viper's smile twisting his lips. "Unless you'd prefer Dad. I know you never had anyone you could call by that name."

It wasn't in her nature to call him what he deserved.

"Preston," she acceded. With that one word, she was out of polite things to say to the man who'd ruined the most important man in her life and who cared little that his son distrusted him.

"Why don't we go have a drink and get to know each other a little better."

Preston caught her by the arm and turned in the direction of Lalique, a stylish two-story bar inside a spectacular three-story crystal chandelier that was Fontaine Chic's centerpiece. Her grandfather hadn't said a word about the three million dollars she'd spent on this single item. Crystal was Violet's signature décor. Throughout the hotel and casino, multifaceted crystals sparkled above the gaming tables and from the fixtures that lined the walkways. Pillars sparkled with embedded lights made to resemble crystals and all the waitresses and dealers wore rhinestone-accented black uniforms.

Preston's firm grip left her feeling very much like a disobedient child being led to her punishment. Annoyed at being manhandled in her own hotel, Violet nonetheless went with JT's father. A scene would harm her more than him and she was certain he knew that. Preston was a master manipulator. It was how he'd gotten the best of his wife's younger brother.

Once they were seated in a quiet table near the railing on the bar's second floor, Preston signaled the waitress. "A bottle of Cristal. We must toast to becoming family."

Violet's skin itched where he'd touched her. The thought of being legally connected to this man, no matter how briefly, made her physically ill.

"I don't drink when I'm working," Violet protested.

"Nonsense. This is a special occasion."

"Then shouldn't we wait to celebrate with JT?"

"My son is running around the country visiting family." Preston's smile didn't reach his hard eyes. "Telling them his good news, I'm assuming." JT's father pinned her with merciless scrutiny. "And yet he left you—his brand-new bride—here. Why is that?"

Again Violet feared her face would betray too much. Tiberius had told her over and over that she made a lousy poker player. She couldn't bluff to save her soul.

"It wasn't a good time for me to be away from the hotel."

"No honeymoon for you then? Stone Properties has a wonderful five-star resort in the Cayman Islands. I could call and have a suite made available for you two."

"Please don't bother."

"It's no bother at all."

The waitress arrived with their champagne and a pair of flutes. Violet appreciated the momentary distraction. She needed to stop reacting and get ahead of Preston. Why had he come? Nothing he did lacked motivation. If he knew JT was traveling, he'd shown up in Vegas to catch Violet alone. Anxiety flared, but she pushed it down. No matter how vile the man, he was powerless to do more than intimidate her.

Once the champagne was poured, Preston handed her a flute. "To wedded bliss. May your life with my son be as happy as mine was with his mother."

More a curse than a blessing, Violet thought as she put the flute to her lips and wet them with the champagne. "Thank you." She set the glass down. "Now, if you'll excuse me, I really have some pressing matters to attend to." But before she could rise, Preston covered her hand with his.

"How long have you and my son been together?"

"A while."

"You must be good at keeping secrets because your wedding caught everyone by surprise."

"JT's very private." And for once she was glad. "We

run rival hotels. He wanted to maintain a low profile until we were sure of our relationship."

"You certainly managed that. No one had a clue that you and he were dating, much less falling in love." Preston leaned forward, his eyes intense. "You are in love with my son, aren't you?"

Violet hesitated before answering. Preston knew something was not on the up and up between her and JT. She saw the challenge in his gaze as if daring her to lie.

"JT is the most amazing man I know. How could I not be?"

That she didn't answer the question directly wasn't lost on Preston. His calculated smile was back.

"And I'm sure he feels the same way about you. I'm glad. I would hate for you to have married him for the wrong reasons."

"Such as?" The instant she spoke, Violet knew she should have insisted she loved JT.

"For his money."

Violet raised her eyebrow and glanced around her. "Do I look like I need money?"

"From what I understand, all this belongs to Fontaine Resorts and Hotels, not to you."

"Regardless, I don't need JT's money."

"That's good." Preston finished his glass of champagne and stood. "I'm very protective of my son. If I thought someone intended to hurt him, I would take steps to see that didn't happen."

She couldn't believe what Preston was saying. He'd done more to hurt his son than the entire rest of the world combined. "I have no plans to hurt JT. Quite the opposite."

"Good. So are you planning on giving up your suite here and moving to my son's ranch?"

Again he'd caught her unprepared. "We haven't decided yet."

"Because two people living apart isn't much of a marriage."

"We'll figure it out."

"And soon, I hope. Because if you're not living together, someone might assume that your marriage is a fake and that would lead to questions."

The entire conversation had been charged with subtext and Violet grew more concerned with each exchange. She suspected Preston had figured out she and JT weren't a love match. Not that there was anything he could do about it.

"Why would anyone care?"

"I care." Preston at last dropped all pretense of being civil. "I know why he married you. To get at the stock Tiberius bought. Well, that only gives him forty-eight percent. Not enough to challenge me."

The speed at which JT's father had figured out what they were up to startled Violet. And yet, should it? The man was devious. He would see a game being played from a mile away. How were they going to get ahead of him if he anticipated all their moves?

"You look worried, Violet."

Preston obviously enjoyed having the upper hand and rubbing his opponent's nose in the fact.

Composing her expression, Violet replied, "I have nothing to be worried about."

"Because you and JT didn't get married so he could use the stock Tiberius left you to stage a coup against me?"

Goose bumps broke out on Violet's arms, but she kept her gaze locked on Preston's cold, flat eyes. "I have no idea what you're talking about."

"Of course you do and when I prove that you two aren't married in good faith, I'm going to sue you for fraud and take back the stock in your possession."

"You can't do that."

"Maybe. Maybe not. But I can tie up the stock in a lawsuit long enough to get rid of my son the same way I got rid of my brother-in-law."

While Violet sat in stunned silence, unsure if she'd ever experienced this level of malice, Preston topped off the champagne in her glass and stood.

"Drink up, Violet. You and my son have embarked on a grand adventure. I only hope you know what you've gotten yourself into."

Preston strolled away before Violet could wrap her thoughts around his threat. Her phone buzzed and she checked the message. JT's plane had just landed at the airport. He had news.

Well…she texted back, agreeing to meet at his house in an hour…so did she.

The drive from Las Vegas to his desert ranch had never bothered JT before. But then again, he'd never had a woman like Violet to come home to either. He banished the thought the instant it entered his head. This was a business meeting. Simple as that.

Violet had used the garage door remote he'd given her and let herself in. He found her curled up on the couch in the living room, staring at the cold fireplace. He had to say her name twice before she realized she was no longer alone. There was a split second of utter delight in her eyes before she frowned.

"You look exhausted. Sit down and let me get you some tea."

"I'd rather have a beer."

"The tea will relax you and soothe your nerves."

"The beer will have the same effect, plus I prefer the way it tastes."

"Fine." When she returned, she held two bottles.

He raised his eyebrow as she handed him one, and she shrugged. "You really shouldn't drink alone."

It was on the tip of his tongue to remind her that he drank alone all the time, but decided not to push her away. Instead, he held out his free hand and pulled her down onto the couch beside him. She landed close and he slung his arm over the back of the couch above her shoulder. Her body fit nicely against his side. He sipped his beer and sighed.

"How's your week going?" he asked, resisting the urge to nuzzle his nose into her silky hair. She'd taken it down and it cascaded around her shoulders in soft waves.

"Until an hour ago, better than yours. You had no luck at all with your family?"

Her first comment snagged his attention. "What happened an hour ago?"

She tensed, and didn't immediately answer. Perplexed, JT glanced down at her. She was staring hard at the beer bottle.

"Violet?" he prompted, growing uneasy.

"We have a problem."

Keeping a sudden flare of concern from his voice, he asked, "What sort of problem?"

"Your father knows what we're doing."

JT cursed silently. "How do you know that?"

"Because he came to see me at Fontaine Chic. He basically told me if he finds out that our marriage isn't real that he'll sue us for fraud."

Fury held him immobile. How dare his father threaten Violet. This was a battle between businessmen. But JT should have been prepared for this. It wasn't the first time Preston Rhodes had intimidated someone who tried to take him on.

"I'll deal with him." JT took a healthy swallow of his beer and swallowed his irritation. No need to get Violet any more worked up than she already was. This wasn't her fight. It was his. That his father chose to confront Violet instead of him let JT know that he was feeling threatened. "It's just a threat to distract us while he shores up support amongst the other shareholders."

"But he said that it would tie up the stock until after the August stockholders' meeting. And that if he keeps control of the company he's going to do to you what he did to Tiberius."

As threats went, it lacked teeth. "There's no immediate family to turn against me," JT reminded her. "As for ejecting me from the company, I was ready to go out on my own before we found out about Tiberius buying stock." JT liked her fierce defense of him. It gave him an urgent need to pull her into his arms and offer her his ardent thanks. "Besides, if he wanted me gone, he could make that happen at any time. He hasn't. He doesn't want to risk losing the support of what shareholders he has at the moment."

"I suppose." She didn't look convinced. "But why should we risk the lawsuit and your reputation when there's a simple solution."

JT grew apprehensive when he realized she'd concocted a plan in that nimble brain of hers. "And that is?"

"We appear as if we're truly married. I'll move in here. We'll let ourselves be seen around town looking like lovebirds. Meanwhile you keep talking to your family."

A simple solution? Maybe on the surface. Definitely for her. But with Violet living here, JT knew it was only a matter of time before he trampled their bargain and made her his wife for real. And then what? He just let her go in a month? Impossible. Once he made her his, there was no going back.

"Sounds perfect," he heard himself say and wondered just how long it would remain so.

* * *

Beneath Scarlett's watchful eye, Violet packed a suitcase full of essentials and ignored most of her sister's questions.

"At least tell me this," Scarlett said. "Are you going to give the man a chance to rock your world?"

Violet sat down on the bed beside her sister. "I'm afraid that if I do that by the time we get divorced I'll be madly in love with him."

"But wouldn't it be worth discovering he's madly in love with you, too?"

"JT's right. Your happiness with Logan makes you want everyone else to find love." Violet shook her head. "It's not where JT and I are heading."

"You're just afraid. Before Logan, I was afraid, too. But trusting him—trusting myself—let me see with my heart as well as my head. All I'm suggesting is that you do the same thing."

"JT doesn't want to let me in. Trying to get to know him is like slogging through mud. Forward progress is slow and exhausting."

"But it's still progress."

"And what if I do get to know him only to discover that he's been damaged so badly he won't be able to accept love much less return it."

"If anyone can fix him, that person is you."

Scarlett's faith strengthened Violet. Was it possible that what had started out as an inspired business strategy could become a viable, satisfying and permanent merger?

"We're having a party at JT's ranch on Tuesday. I need you, Logan and Harper to come for moral support."

"Of course we'll come, but you don't really need us. You and JT will do great together. I think you make a wonderful team. I'll bet Tiberius did too. It's probably why he left the stock to you instead of to JT with the caveat that you couldn't dispose of it until far in the future."

Ever since the reading of his will, Violet had wondered about Tiberius's motivation for doing so as well. Why had he given her the stock and forced her to hold on to it knowing that she wouldn't be able to vote?

Plagued by questions she'd never know the answer to, Violet drove to JT's ranch and arrived at three in the afternoon. JT's housekeeper took charge of Violet's luggage and informed her that JT was in the barn. Curious, Violet went in search of him.

To describe JT's property as a ranch was a little misleading. What he had was a first-class training facility for show horses. The barn was a state-of-the-art structure with an impressive lobby whose walls were lined with large photos of expensive-looking horses doing dressage or jumping fences. The centerpiece of the room was a large bronze horse and female rider. Violet wondered if it had been modeled after JT's grandmother.

Off the lobby were several offices, currently empty. A door toward the back had a sign on it that indicated it led to the barn. Violet pushed her way through. She expected to be hit with heat, noise and stench, but it was a comfortable eighty degrees, and the few sounds that reached her ear were muted crunching and an occasional nose clearing. As for the smell, whatever air conditioning JT had incorporated into his design also pulled the dust from the air as well as the strongest of the horsey odors of hay, sweat and manure.

The concrete floor between the stalls was newly swept and free of dust. Violet wandered along, peering into stalls as she went. With each step she took, she found herself growing more and more calm. By the time she rounded a corner and spotted JT, down on one knee, wrapping some sort of poultice around a horse's knee, she was humming.

"Hi," she said, stopping ten feet from the large horse.

JT glanced up at her greeting and offered her a lopsided grin that made her heart jerk almost painfully. He wore camel-colored jodhpurs and knee-high boots. A navy polo shirt showed off the strong column of his throat and his powerful biceps.

"I'll be just a couple minutes more, then I can give you a tour of the place."

"Take your time."

She was enjoying the view. After not seeing JT for five days, she'd almost been able to convince herself that the way she'd melted beneath his kisses had been a symptom of her shock at learning what Tiberius had left her and reaction to her impulsive and speedy wedding. Then he'd returned and she'd proposed that they move in together. She could deny her feelings to Harper and Scarlett, but it was a lot harder to lie to herself.

She was hoping the chemistry between her and JT would combust and land them in bed together. Admitting it made her giddy. She'd disavowed the truth long enough. She wanted JT Stone in a big way and her subconscious had positioned her perfectly to act on those feelings.

"You ready?"

While she'd been coming to grips with her desires, JT had finished with the horse and a groom was leading it away.

"Sure."

JT guided her down the row of stalls, telling her a little bit about all the different horses.

"Until I stepped into the barn, I didn't realize this was a training facility," she exclaimed as he opened one of the stall doors and stepped inside. "How many horses do you have here?"

"We have fifty in training. They're all housed on this side. Across the arena is a whole other line of stalls where we keep horses for sale and the mares who are either in foal or who have babies. There's another forty over there."

"So, this is much more than a hobby for you."

"Not really. Vic manages the facility and deals with all the clients. Ralph is in charge of the training. Sid handles the sales. Bonnie keeps everyone healthy and watches over the mares. The place doesn't need me to run."

But from the way everyone they met asked his opinion or updated him on the barn's occupants, she gathered he was the heart and soul of the operation.

"This is Milo." JT laughed as they approached a stall and he had to push the horse's nose away from his pocket. "You get treats after you work, not before."

"Is he yours?"

"No. He belongs to a very talented ten-year-old girl. I've been his trainer for two years."

Keeping her gaze off her husband's handsome face— relaxed and unguarded for the first time she'd noticed— was necessary to avoid embarrassing herself with renewed pleas for his kisses. Instead, Violet stared at the horse. His back was well over five and a half feet off the ground. "A little girl rides this horse? That's a long way to fall."

"She's been riding since she was three. She has an amazing seat. The sort my grandmother had. And a real feel for the horse. She and Milo are quite a team. She'll be by for a lesson tomorrow. You can see for yourself."

"I'd like that."

JT slipped a halter over the horse's head and led him out of the stall. He held the lead rope out to her. "Can you hold him for me while I get my saddle and bridle?"

"Me?" She squeaked out the word after sizing up the enormous animal. "I've never handled a horse before."

"He's a big pussycat." JT put the rope in her hands. The horse took a step toward her, his ears forward. "Blow lightly into his nostril. He likes it and it will help you two get acquainted."

If it had been anyone but JT she might have assumed she was being pranked. Still, she felt silly following his instructions until the big horse pricked his ears and breathed back at her. On some sort of horse level they were communicating. By the time JT returned with a saddle and bridle, she had grown brave enough to pet the horse's soft nose and scratch his cheek.

"Looks like you two have hit it off," JT observed, setting the saddle carefully on the floor. He held out a brush. "Feel like giving me a hand?"

"Sure." She sounded more confident than she felt, but as she applied the brush to the animal's rich brown coat, she was overcome by a sense of peace. No wonder JT enjoyed his horses. Being with them grounded him firmly in the moment. Nothing mattered but the stroke of a brush against Milo's warm flank. It was the perfect counterpoint to the Las Vegas strip. "It's very Zen," she remarked.

"This is where I spend my days. I can handle just about any crisis after a few hours with the horses."

JT tossed the saddle onto Milo's back and fastened the cinch. While he worked, he spoke softly to the horse. Mostly nonsense, but it was his melodious tone that the horse listened and responded to. And he wasn't the only one. Violet found herself lulled as well.

"Can you hand me his bridle?"

His question snapped her out of her trance. Spending time with him like this meant she risked falling beneath JT's spell. Eventually, reality would intrude and she'd be in too deep. She just had to decide if getting hurt was worth the ride.

"Here you go."

The horse stood patiently while JT slipped off the halter and replaced it with the bridle. His actions were smooth and efficient. Remembering Scarlett's opinion about JT's hands, Violet watched as he fastened buckles, double-checked the fit of the cinch and soothed the horse with a stroke along his shoulder. By the time JT turned the horse toward the door that led into the arena, Violet was experiencing waves of heat that had nothing to do with the air temperature.

"You can watch me work Milo from there." JT pointed to the far corner where several chairs sat on a raised platform. He handed her a small towel. "We use crumb rubber as a footing to keep down the dust, but you'll probably want to wipe off the chair."

She glanced down at her flat sandals and pale blue skirt. "I guess I'm not really dressed for the barn, am I? If I'm going to visit in the future, I'd better wear jeans."

"And boots as well. Not everyone is as careful where they put their feet as Milo. I wouldn't want your pretty toes crushed."

"You think I have pretty toes?" His offhanded compliment made her grin.

His eyes glowed as he gave her a quick once-over. "I think you have pretty everything."

It was on the tip of her tongue to shoot back that he hadn't seen her everything, but then she recalled how he'd caught her skinny-dipping. At the time, he'd been so annoyed, it hadn't occurred to her to wonder how much he'd seen. Now, she suspected he'd glimpsed more than he let on.

"JT…" She had no idea how to convey what she wanted without giving away too much.

"Don't read too much into that," he told her. "You're beautiful. I find you attractive. It doesn't mean I can't control myself around you."

His words acted like an ice bath. "I'm not sure whether to be insulted or relieved."

Teeth flashing in a wry grin, JT led Milo to the center of the arena, leaving her standing in an emotional stew of her own making. When she'd set out to discover JT's true identity, the one a painful childhood had forced into hiding, she'd done so thinking that it would do him good to connect with people.

But after seeing the way he related to his barn staff and the joy he received from working with the horses, she realized he wasn't the damaged train wreck she'd assumed. He had a healthy outlet for his passion. A place of peace that benefited others. He wasn't exactly the loner she perceived him as—and felt sorry for. What else had she gotten wrong?

As Violet watched JT swing his long lean form into the saddle, she felt her perceptions shift. Her ego had fooled her into believing JT needed her when it was so obvious that he had things all figured out. He didn't need her to run to his rescue with a marriage of convenience or to draw him out of his shell for his own good. He'd been doing just fine on his own. Yet he'd accepted her help. It wasn't as if anyone could force JT to do something he didn't want to do.

Milo moved through a series of maneuvers that looked complex, but which the horse executed with ease. JT sat quietly in the saddle, appearing on first glance to be more passenger than active participant. But his concentration told a different story. Violet paid closer attention to his hands and legs. Still she couldn't discern what JT was doing to make the horse side-pass one direction for a few steps and then abruptly switch and go the other way.

JT was asking the horse to dance for him. His control over the animal was amazing. And sexy as hell.

After fifteen minutes he dropped the reins onto Milo's neck and patted the horse on both shoulders. His broad grin made Violet catch her breath. So this was what it felt like to swoon over a guy. She'd never experienced anything like it and wasn't sure how to behave now that her body had a mind of its own.

"That was amazing," Violet called, stepping off the platform.

JT dismounted and led Milo toward her. He stroked the horse's neck. "He did all the work." A slight sheen had developed on JT's forehead, contradicting his assertion.

"I don't believe that."

Their eyes connected and locked. JT's smile faded. What had been warm flesh a moment earlier became solid granite, and Violet's heart sank as she watched the doors slam shut over his thoughts. After several heartbeats, JT sucked in a deep lungful of air.

"I lied to you earlier," he said, his gaze probing hers, searching for answers, but giving nothing away.

The disappointment she'd felt seconds earlier faded slightly as her heartbeat accelerated beneath his intent expression. "About what?"

"About—"

"If you're all done with Milo, Boss, I can take him." A groom stepped into the arena. "Bonnie is in with Bullet and wonders if you can come look at the foal. She's wondering if we should call the vet."

"You're busy," Violet said, taking a half step back. "And I promised Harper I'd come in early today so we could discuss a joint promotion." As excuses went, it wasn't the best, but she needed time to regroup and figure out what she really wanted from JT before things started to happen. "We can talk after work tonight."

He caught her arm and kept her from moving away. The groom was fast approaching. Violet's heart thumped hard against her ribs as JT lowered his lips toward her ear.

"Your sister was right," he murmured, his warm breath sliding seductively over her skin. "I am hungry for you."

And then he was handing Milo off to the groom and striding away from her. Violet stared after him, her knees pressed together for stability because the strength had gone out of her muscles.

He was hungry for her?

He was hungry for her.

Well, that was good because she was hungry for him as well.

Seven

The ranch house was quiet and dark when JT let himself in at two in the morning. He'd cut his night short, unable to concentrate on business with thoughts of Violet bombarding him. He liked that she'd shown up at the barn today. Watching her overcome her anxiety about Milo had demonstrated that her interest had been genuine. Having her gaze follow his every move in the arena had been a pleasant distraction. He'd stepped up his game and showed off for her like a smitten teenage boy.

What he'd seen in her eyes made him want to throw her over his shoulder and carry her straight to his bedroom. Was she reconsidering the arrangement? He hoped so. But if she needed more convincing, he was ready for that as well.

Taking the stairs two at a time, JT headed down the hall to her bedroom. The door stood ajar, the room beyond dark. He let his eyes adjust and saw that the room was unoccupied. Reaching in, he flipped on the light. The room wasn't just empty. It showed no sign that anyone was staying there.

If JT hadn't seen Violet's car in the garage, he would've

assumed that she'd changed her mind and returned to Fontaine Chic. Perhaps she'd chosen a different room. There were four others she might prefer. But none showed signs of life. So where was she?

JT headed for the terrace outside the master suite. As soon as he stepped outside he heard the sound of splashing. She'd gone for a swim. He grabbed a set of swim trunks from a drawer and changed. It wasn't until he entered the closet to hang up his suit that he realized which bedroom she'd decided to sleep in.

His.

What had once been the empty half of the enormous his-and-hers closet was now filled with black dresses, casual daytime wear and several pairs of jeans. The shoe racks overflowed with pumps and sandals. He returned to the bedroom and discovered half his drawers filled with lacy lingerie, knit tops and scarves. The countertop in his bathroom bore perfume bottles and creams.

Holy hell.

He marched down the stairs at a deliberate pace, formulating how to approach Violet about this new development. It was one thing to perpetuate the myth of their happy marriage by living together. But sharing his room—his bed—with her was taking the playacting way too far.

JT stalked through the living room and stepped onto the pool deck. Violet stroked through the water, naked limbs breaking the surface and plunging back in again. Damn, but she was beautiful. Her movements were lazy, content. The exact opposite of the riotous emotions surging through JT.

He was standing at the edge of the pool before he even realized he'd moved. "I found all your things in my room. What's going on?"

"I got to thinking your dad might have spies in your employ. I don't want to give him any ammunition against you." She didn't meet his gaze, which made him wonder what she had to hide.

"I think you're giving him too much credit."

"Come for a swim. We can talk about it later."

He wanted to get it resolved right now. JT dove in and swam underwater toward her. With just the pool lights to see by, he didn't realize that she was naked until he was close enough to touch her.

He came up coughing.

"Are you all right?" She set her hands on his shoulders and peered at him.

"I thought we had an understanding about your skinny-dipping."

To his immense shock, she hooked her fingertips into the elastic waistband of his swim trunks and pulled it a couple inches away from his stomach. Her touch against his bare skin brought him to a swift and fierce arousal. He clenched his teeth to contain a groan.

"You should try it," she murmured, her smile come-hither. A second later he felt the snap against his belly as she let go. In a flash she was gone. Water splashed against his cheeks and blinded him as she dove sideways, swimming beyond his grasp in seconds.

Sputtering, he shook his head to clear his eyes and took off after her with a growl. It wasn't until he caught her at the edge of the pool and pinned her against the wall that he remembered she was naked. Her thighs tangled with his and she hooked one foot around his calf to anchor herself to him.

"Kiss me," she demanded, sliding her palms up the side of his neck and latching onto his hair. "Soft, slow, hard, deep. I don't care. Just make me lose myself."

His lips captured hers in a relentless assault that definitively declared that this time there would be no backpedaling, no stopping, no mercy. She accepted every stroke of his tongue, every nip of his teeth and gave him back frenzied desire and impatience. Her nails bit into his skin, her moans heightened his already explosive hunger. She writhed against him, her hips moving rhythmically against his erection, driving him wild.

He sucked the water from her neck, tasting chlorine and below that the sweetness of her skin. His breath caught as she threw her head back and offered him even more access. He wrapped his fingers around her delicate ribcage and lifted her until her perfect breasts bobbed above the water's surface. She wrapped her thighs around his waist as he locked his mouth over one hard nipple. With her wet heat pressed tight to his abdomen, he sucked and nibbled first one breast, then the other until her breath came in short, tight pants.

Her lithe body trembled in his arms as he grazed his fingertips down her spine and splayed his hands over the firm planes of her butt. She'd been working her hips in an ever-increasing rhythm. What she wanted, she wasn't getting and she unhooked her ankles from around his waist and let her feet drift to the pool bottom.

Once again he felt her tug on his trunks. This time she forced the fabric downward, freeing his erection. He hissed through his teeth as the pool water hit the sensitive head. The sound was followed a second later by his strangled moan as she closed her fingers around his hard length.

He slammed his mouth down over hers, plunging his tongue inward, all technique lost in the savage need to claim her. She matched his kiss with sweet ferocity, using her tongue and teeth to drive him wild.

"Give it all to me," she murmured, stroking him in ever more tantalizing sweeps as he sucked on her neck.

She parted her thighs and placed the tip of him at her entrance. He nudged firmly against her hot wet core, and almost cried out at the agony of holding back, but remained perfectly still.

"Protection," he garbled out the word, unsure how he was going let her go, walk all the way upstairs and fetch a condom from his nightstand.

"I'm on the pill." She arched her back and rocked her hips forward, embedding him inside her before her words fully registered.

The tightness of her encased him and nothing JT had ever dreamed of matched the reality of Violet naked and in his arms. He put his hands on her hips and settled himself deeper still, hanging onto his control for dear life so he could make the moment into something they would both find satisfying.

"You are amazing," he murmured as they rocked together in the pool, stirring the water as they kissed and caressed.

Time slowed. JT's world narrowed to the rush of air through his lungs, the surge of heat in his groin and the warm silk of Violet's skin caressing his.

"This is so much better than I imagined it would be," she whispered, her breath tickling his ear.

"You thought about it?"

He wandered his hands over her back and down her thighs as his lips drifted along her shoulder. She'd locked the soles of her feet against his calves to anchor herself in the weightlessness of the water. It gave her the leverage to add a little twisting motion to the rhythmic movements of her hips. The power of that move was close to blowing a hole in his willpower. He ground his teeth against a groan.

"Night and day since you first started showing up at Baccarat."

Her confession prompted him to offer one of his own. "Losing Rick to you was the best thing that ever happened to me."

"You don't say." Her chest vibrated with a sexy laugh, making her breasts shift tantalizingly against him. Her tight nipples were searing points of heat that quickened his breath.

"Or it was," he amended, unable to stave off the quickening of sensations any longer. "Until now."

He moved more strongly into her and felt her close tightly around him, forming a tight sheath. The friction was almost too intense to handle. But if her body brought him acute pleasure, her dreamy smile was a balm for his spirit.

And then he felt her body tighten and her focus sharpen. Using all his willpower to hold off his own release, he watched her climb higher and higher. Her eyes flew open. Her sharp gasp was followed by a shudder. Only then did JT let himself go.

His orgasm came with such speed and intensity he wondered how he'd held it off as long as he had. The pool, Violet's face, all vanished behind a wave of black. He was cast into the heavens. A thousand pinpoints of lights guided his flight. They rushed at him, through him. Each one left a mark, a permanent reminder of this perfect moment.

He came back to earth and realized that his chest hurt. The pain was caused by either his tortured lungs or the impossibly swift beat of his heart.

"Best sex ever," Violet murmured, framing his face with her hands and smiling at him. Equally winded, she seemed less shaken by their turbulent lovemaking. "I knew it would be great with you, but wow."

He couldn't match her openness. What he felt for her was too immense, too raw.

"Yes." It wasn't eloquent, but it was heartfelt. "Wow."

The corners of her eyes crinkled as her grin grew. "Am I still banned from skinny-dipping?"

Captivated by her happiness, he shook his head. "In fact, I plan to burn every bathing suit in the place."

* * *

"You're smiling a lot this morning," Harper commented, eyeing Violet over a glass of orange juice.

It was Tuesday morning and the Fontaine sisters were meeting for their weekly breakfast, this morning in Scarlett's office at Fontaine Richesse. Usually they met on Wednesdays, but Violet and JT were having their belated wedding reception at the ranch that evening and they all figured it would be a late night.

"Am I?" Violet sipped her green tea and tried to look nonchalant.

"Of course she's smiling," Scarlett put in. "She and JT have been shacked up for three days of postnuptial bliss."

"I don't think it can be called 'shacked up' if we're married," Violet corrected her.

Harper frowned in confusion. "You're living together now?"

"If you'd pay attention to something other than your hotel once in a while," Scarlett began, "you'd know that Preston showed up here and threatened to sue JT and Violet for fraud if their marriage wasn't real."

"He can't possibly have a case," Harper said.

Scarlett smirked. "Not anymore."

"What I mean," Harper continued, shooting Scarlett a look, "is there's nothing in the corporate bylaws insisting the marriage must be real, just legal."

"We were concerned that by taking us to court, he could prevent me from voting my shares at the upcoming shareholder meeting and remain CEO."

A line formed between Harper's brows. "I guess that's possible. I just don't know how likely."

"We didn't want to take the chance."

"And because of that your relationship has become physical?"

Violet resisted looking Scarlett's way for fear that her

sister's expression would make her laugh. Harper was a little too literal and that often kept her from finding the humor in a situation.

"Not exactly…"

"He's crazy about her and vice versa," Scarlett explained. "Unlike you and Ashton where you make each other crazy."

"I have every right to be crazy," Harper insisted. "The restaurant is behind schedule because he hasn't been here to make decisions. And when he does make decisions, it puts us even more behind schedule because he wants to change things."

Scarlett gave her sister a doubting look. "To say nothing of the fact that he's gorgeous and sexy and your DVR is full of his television series."

Harper's scowl would have been more intimidating if she'd been able to meet Scarlett's gaze. "It seems to me that you and Logan were in that drive-each-other-crazy place less than a month ago."

Scarlett and her security-expert fiancé were so madly in love these days it was hard to remember just how much they used to antagonize each other

"That was then. Now we just drive each other crazy with passion."

Harper's response was a rude noise. Violet chuckled. She loved her sisters. To outsiders, it sometimes appeared as if the three of them didn't get along, but in fact for three women who'd not known each other until their grandfather introduced them five years ago, they were as tight as siblings who'd grown up together. Maybe even tighter because there were no childhood battle scars.

"Putting aside all the *crazy* talk for a second," Violet said, turning to Scarlett, "you said you had something important you wanted to discuss with me."

After some meaningful eye contact with Harper, Scarlett went to her desk and brought back two files. She held one suspended in Violet's direction and said, "I know I've told you a little about the files I inherited from Tiberius. This one is about Preston Rhodes."

Curious, Violet accepted the file and quickly scanned it. The contents included old newspaper clippings about a flash flood drowning in the desert near Las Vegas as well as a grainy group photo of seven rough-looking young men. Below that was a piece of paper with a woman's name and contact information on it. Charity Rimes.

"What am I looking at?" Violet asked.

"Grady and I think the man we know as Preston Rhodes is actually a local Las Vegas kid who was supposed to have drowned during a flash flood back in 1970."

Violet glanced at Harper and saw in her sister's expression the same skepticism she was feeling. "So, the newspaper report got it wrong? It wasn't this George Barnes guy, but Preston Rhodes. How is that possible?"

"I think JT's father—whose real name I think is George Barnes—switched identities with Preston Rhodes after Preston was killed in the flash flood."

"That's a pretty wild theory," Harper interjected.

"Why would he do that?" Violet wanted to know.

"From what information Tiberius had gathered about George Barnes, he'd been a juvenile delinquent on his way to a bad end. Preston Rhodes had a bright future ahead of him. A rich kid with no family. He'd left California, where he'd grown up, to take a road trip to the East Coast where he would be attending college. Think of how easy it would have been for George to simply step into Preston's shoes."

Violet skimmed the clippings, and realized that Scarlett's explanation was sounding more reasonable by the second. And after meeting JT's father, she had no trouble believing the man was ruthless and unscrupulous enough to steal another man's identity and fortune. But what would this mean for JT? She imagined how devastating this revelation would be to him. Finding out your father had stolen someone's identity was a far cry from merely worrying that he was making poor business decisions.

With her stomach in knots, Violet set aside the file. "I don't know what you want me to do with this."

"You should talk to Charity Rimes. Tiberius tracked her down for a reason."

"Who is she?" Harper asked.

"She's the writer doing a story on a series of killings in Los Angeles back in the sixties. I don't know much about the story other than they never caught the guy. I let the whole matter drop when I realized it wasn't any of my business. But things have changed. JT married you. That makes him family." Scarlett extended a second file. "Which brings me to this. I don't know if you want to read it or not, but since you're now involved with JT, I thought I should at least give you the choice."

"Tiberius had a file on JT." Violet wondered why he hadn't kept it in his home office. "Have you read it?"

"I was tempted to when I first suspected his dad of stealing Preston Rhodes's identity, but then I decided it wasn't my place to know his secrets." She extended the file to Violet.

The amount of paper contained in the manila folder took Violet by surprise. This wasn't a simple summary of his unhappy childhood and adolescent acting out. Tiberius had spent time and energy researching his nephew. Probably in preparation for renewing their relationship.

Reading the file would be a shortcut to learning most everything that had gone into developing JT's character. No doubt she'd learn things about him he wouldn't appreciate her knowing. But maybe talking about the most painful events would help him to heal. And if he healed, perhaps he could then open himself up to love.

As soon as the thought occurred, Violet reined it in. Was she hoping that if she fixed him he'd be so grateful he'd never want their marriage to end? They'd been married less than two weeks and she was already figuring out ways to manipulate him. Better to let JT tell her what he wished her to know when he wanted her to know it.

"I shouldn't." Violet tried to hand the folder back to Scarlett, but she put up her hands.

"Keep it. Burn it. Give it to JT. I don't care, but I don't want it back in my possession." Scarlett glanced at Harper who was glaring at her smartphone. "I'm already the keeper of more secrets than I'm comfortable knowing."

Violet knew Scarlett was referring to the file she'd found on Harper's mother. The one with the potential to turn Harper's life upside down. From her calm demeanor, Violet suspected that Scarlett hadn't yet decided to share with her half sister what was in the file.

"I have to go," Harper said, getting to her feet. "I emailed Ashton another round of head chef candidates and he has fifteen minutes of free time to talk about them."

As soon as Harper left the room, Scarlett fetched another file from her desk. "I wasn't kidding when I said I'm uncomfortable with the secrets I'm keeping."

"Are you planning to tell her what you discovered about her mother?"

"I'm going to tell you what's going on and I want you to help me decide."

"Very well." When Violet had first found out about the file on Harper's mother, she'd sympathized with Scarlett's dilemma. Now she had a similar problem—what to do with the files on JT and his father. "What did Harper's mother do?"

"She had a brief affair during an extended period of time where her husband was away on business."

"Penelope?" Violet couldn't believe Harper's uptight

mother could have done anything that rash. "It's so un-like her."

Scarlett opened the file and displayed the black-and-white photos of a young Penelope Fontaine and a handsome man in a hot embrace.

"Apparently being married to our father could push even the most conservative person into reckless behavior," Scarlett remarked, sounding more tired than wry.

"I'm sure Harper will be shocked and embarrassed by her mother's actions, but it was a long time ago." Violet wanted to reject what her eyes were seeing. "But I don't understand why you think it will devastate her."

"Because she was born nine months later."

It took several seconds for Scarlett's meaning to penetrate. "You mean…?"

"Harper isn't a Fontaine."

"Are you sure?"

"Unfortunately, yes." Scarlett closed her eyes. Pain raced across her features. "How can I tell her that?"

When Harper found out the truth about her parentage, she'd be destroyed.

"I don't think you should," Violet said at last.

Harper had the education and the business savvy to run Fontaine Resorts and Hotels, not to mention the ambition and a seemingly inexhaustible store of energy, and she'd spent her whole life preparing to run the family business. In the last five years Violet had learned enough about Harper's character to guess she'd bow out of the contest to determine the next CEO.

A year ago Violet would have been excited at the prospect of moving into the lead. She had Harper's ambition and drive, of late she'd been thinking less about her career and more about her personal life. The transition had been subtle, but she suspected it had begun around the time JT started showing up at Baccarat.

As for Scarlett, the former child star had recently decided to return part-time to acting. Splitting her time and attention between L.A. and Las Vegas meant she'd already decided not to actively compete for the CEO position. Nor was Violet convinced Scarlett had ever truly given herself props for the work she'd done to make Fontaine Richesse the standout hotel it was.

Scarlett nodded somberly and returned the photos to the file. "It's what I think, too. No good will come of telling her."

With too many secrets weighing her down, Violet left Scarlett's office and headed to her suite to find a dress to wear to her belated wedding reception. She'd been so preoccupied with the details for the party that she'd forgotten all about herself.

In the back of her closet was a pale pink chiffon dress embellished with blush and silver sequins on the bodice. Three years ago, she'd bought it to wear to a charity event that at the last minute she'd been unable to attend. Despite having spent a fortune on the dress and the matching pink slingbacks, Violet couldn't bring herself to return the ensemble. She knew eventually she'd be attending a party where she could wear it. Her wedding reception fit the bill.

As she was exiting her suite, her gaze fell on the files Scarlett had given her. She hadn't decided what to tell JT yet. He'd been through so much already. But she didn't want to go behind his back on something as serious as his father stealing another man's identity. Leaving JT's file on her home office desk, she slipped Preston's and the one containing information on Charity Rimes into her briefcase and exited the suite.

Eight

"You look gorgeous." Impatient for a last minute alone with her, JT linked his fingers with Violet's and tugged her toward the stairs. They had fifteen minutes until their guests were due to arrive.

"Is it silly that I'm nervous?" With her free hand, she smoothed her skirt and tugged at her neckline.

"Yes." He lifted her hand to his lips and kissed her knuckles. "Everyone here tonight will be a friend. And I'll be at your side the entire evening."

To his gratification, she looked reassured. "And you're sure I look okay?"

"You're perfect." He wasn't accustomed to her lack of confidence and wondered how someone as beautiful and charming as Violet could doubt herself.

"Because the dress is three years old."

"It looks brand-new."

"That's because it is. I've never worn it."

The subtleties of a woman's mind when it came to fashion were lost on JT. "Let's go have a glass of champagne. I want to make a toast."

He led her outside to the pool deck. Because of the number of guests who would be coming, they'd opted to open the living room's glass walls so people could enjoy the night air. Tiny white lights decorated the palm trees and shrubs, adding a festive air. A bottle of champagne and two flutes awaited them in the outdoor seating area.

JT popped the cork and poured the sparkling liquid. He handed one to Violet and cleared his throat.

"To you. Thank you for marrying me. It's been a long time since anyone has acted in my best interests instead of their own. Your optimism and knack for thinking outside the box have enabled me to shake loose the cobwebs and let in the sunlight. No matter what happens a month from now, I am ready for whatever the future brings."

The toast was awkward and sappy, but Violet didn't seem to notice. Her eyes remained riveted on him as he spoke. Her faith had given him wings. His father could throw every vile trick in the book his way and JT would let it all roll off him. It was impossible to convey the depth of his appreciation for all Violet had given him.

"I'm glad to hear you say that," Violet told him, clinking her glass to his. "And I hope I can continue to make good things happen for you."

"All I need is for you—"

"There's the couple of the hour," a man announced from the living room. It was Brent. He'd flown in from Charlotte earlier that day and was staying at Titanium.

Fighting back a sigh at the interruption, JT towed his wife to greet his cousin. After introductions were made, JT caught a subtle nod of approval from Brent and relaxed. His cousin's opinion mattered. Everyone else could go to hell.

Shortly after Brent's arrival, the floodgates opened and guests began to pour in. In addition to family and friends, they'd invited many business associates from Las Vegas. Waitstaff circled with glasses of champagne and fancy hors d'oeuvres. With the help of her catering manager, Violet had organized the party within a week and the entire evening flowed without a hitch. And with each hour that passed, JT found himself a little more enthralled with his wife.

She charmed everyone with her quick laugh and positive outlook. He was glad the evening called for them to navigate the room as a couple, because he couldn't bring himself to move more than an arm's length away.

The floral scent she wore made his head spin with shameless thoughts of what he intended to do with her later. He had a hard time keeping his hands off her bare arms.

"You've been monopolizing your wife the whole evening," Scarlett complained, tugging Violet away. "Harper and I need a couple minutes with her."

JT continued to move about the room, but what little enjoyment he'd had in the evening had been leached away the second Violet had gone. More than anything he wished everyone would just go home.

After what seemed like hours, but had been no more than fifteen minutes, Violet returned to him.

"I missed you," he murmured, after welcoming her with a quick kiss.

By the end of the night, he accepted that he was the luckiest man in the world. As they stood in the doorway and bid the last of their guests goodbye, JT became aware of a raging need to have her all to himself. The instant she closed the front door and let out an enormous sigh of relief, he lifted her onto his shoulder and headed upstairs.

At first she was too startled to protest, but she'd rediscovered her voice by the time he reached the second floor.

"Have you lost your mind? There are still things to clean up and I need to thank the caterer. Put me down."

"She left twenty minutes ago. You and I are all alone." He deposited her on the king-size bed in the master suite. "Finally."

"We've been alone these last four days," she reminded him, sliding his shirt buttons free.

He tugged the thin strap off her shoulder and buried his face in her neck. Her scent had been driving him crazy all night. It reminded him of two days ago when he'd...

JT's brain short-circuited. Her busy hands had unfastened his zipper and slipped inside his pants to cup him. He groaned, his erection growing impossibly hard beneath her clever touch.

"Slow down," he commanded, snagging her wrists and pinning them onto the pillows above her head. "We have all night."

"But I need you now." She slowly gyrated her hips in the way she knew made him crazy. "And we're both ready. Why can't you just go with it?"

Because he'd been *going with it* for four days and had yet to learn all he wanted to about pleasing her. Their chemistry was so explosive. He'd never been with anyone like her. Eager, passionate, sexy as hell. She could look at him from across the room and he'd want her. His obsession grew worse every day. It interfered with his ability to focus at work and distracted him from the purpose of their marriage in the first place: gaining the stock he needed to oust his father.

"You want me to go with it?" he asked, rolling off the bed so he could strip off his shirt, pants and underwear.

"Very much." She watched him with greedy eyes as she got to her knees and stripped off her fancy cocktail dress. Clad in a strapless bra and silk bikini underwear, she waited for him in the middle of the bed, her hands on her hips in brazen challenge.

"Very well." His smile acknowledged that if she wanted to play, he could too. "Turn and face the headboard."

Surprise and uncertainty flickered in her eyes for a

moment, but after a short hesitation she did as he asked. Peering at him over her shoulder, she asked, "Like this?"

"Just like that."

He moved onto the bed and came up behind her. Her beautiful back was a feature he'd not had much opportunity to explore these past few days and it was worth his attention. The first thing he did was pop the catch on her bra so he could appreciate her delicate spine without hindrance.

The elastic that held the bra in place had created indentations on her skin. He bent his head and kissed the marks while drawing his fingertips along her narrow shoulders. She quivered beneath his light touch and her breath hissed out in a long sigh.

Little by little she relaxed as his fingers explored the contours of her shoulder blades, lightly massaged her nape and drifted down her arms. As he sucked on the place where her neck and shoulder came together, she leaned back against him and savored the prod of his erection against her butt.

"That's nice," she murmured, arms straight at her sides, palms resting on his thighs. "But what can I do for you?"

"Enjoy this. That's all I ask."

Violet didn't ask what *this* was. She was feeling lazy and aroused. Her skin was delighted to receive all the consideration JT was lavishing on it. Despite the insistent throbbing between her thighs, she hoped he'd treat her entire body to the same attention to detail.

"You have a beautiful back. I love the dimples right here." He pointed out the particular spot with a soft caress.

"You know there's a whole 'nother side of me that would love some attention."

He kissed her neck. "Such as?"

"My breasts."

Following her command, he grazed his palms up her sides. She caught her breath as his long fingers stroked across her sensitive nipples, and exhaled as he swallowed her fullness in his hands.

"Better?"

"Much."

"Where else would you like me to touch you?"

She sucked her lower lip between her teeth and bit down as his hands moved over her abdomen and caressed the tops of her thighs. She rotated her hips as the ache built deep in her loins. Undulating waves of longing pulsed through her.

"Here."

Shaking with need, she snagged his strong hands and urged them toward her mound. He'd knelt with his knees on either side of hers. Now, he nudged her thighs apart, spreading her legs wide, opening her. She gulped at the brush of cool air against her tender flesh. Anticipation of his possession aroused her still more until she thought she'd go mad with longing.

"JT, this is not fair."

"What's not fair?"

He turned her face toward him and rubbed his lips over hers, mingling their breath, but not giving her the satisfaction of his tongue. She wanted a deep, penetrating kiss. Something to momentarily take her mind off the painful throbbing at her core.

"You aren't taking advantage of having me in this position."

"No?" He nipped at her neck. "What should I be doing?"

She wagged her hips, rubbing herself against his erection. He groaned. At last his fingers slid into the cleft between her thighs. She almost cried out at the pleasure.

"You're so hot," he muttered, his tone guttural and low. "It makes me crazy how wet you get."

"Show me." She bent forward at the waist and let her hands fall to the mattress.

From between his teeth came a savage curse. JT seized her hips and in one swift move plunged into her. The position offered Violet a whole new range of sensation and she released a soft "oh" of surprise.

JT kissed her back. "Are you okay?"

"Wonderful. Perfect." She sucked in a breath and laughed. "In fact, it's fabulous. Keep going."

Snorting his amusement, JT began rocking against her. Faster than Violet would have imagined, she felt an orgasm rising to meet her. And when JT reached between her thighs and plucked at the knot of nerves, she went off like a rocket.

"Yes!"

JT picked up his pace and continued to fondle her. To Violet's intense shock, she didn't settle to earth on a golden cloud like normal, but felt another pulse of pleasure stab her. She quaked as her second climax roared through her.

Before she had a chance to marvel at the wonder of it all, JT dove into her hard two more times and was claimed by his own release. He collapsed onto her back, his chest vibrating with laughter.

Catching her around the waist, he shifted his weight and rolled them onto the mattress. They landed in a tangle of limbs. JT pushed himself up so he could peer into her face. He had to brush her hair away from her eyes before he could meet her gaze.

"Did you just come twice?" he demanded in amazement.

She grinned. "I believe I did."

"You are the most incredible woman I've ever been with."

His words were sweet music to her ears. She'd never had a man appreciate her lovemaking the way JT did. And the feeling was mutual. He made her feel like a goddess.

It was heady stuff for a girl who'd too often been self-conscious in bed.

"It's only because you're such a wonderful lover."

He sobered. "Don't do that."

"Do what?" She couldn't imagine what she'd said to make him look so unhappy.

"Downplay how terrific you are."

She squirmed a little beneath his intense regard. "I get uncomfortable when anyone says nice things about me."

"Why is that?"

"I guess I don't always believe that I deserve it."

"That's ridiculous."

She lifted one shoulder and let it fall. "Ever since I was three, I knew my father didn't want to have anything to do with me. I thought that was my fault."

"But you know it wasn't."

It was easier to talk about her insecurities when she was staring at his chin. His outraged expression made her feel even worse. "These days, sure. But it hurt for a long time and I forged some armor that I wear when I'm feeling vulnerable."

"You don't need to wear it around me."

He kissed her with reverent gentleness, endeavoring to heal her hurts with tenderness. Violet's chest ached. Falling deep in love with him was so easy when he offered her his support like this. But she couldn't help but be saddened by the fact that he wouldn't let her help him in kind.

In the calm after their earlier passion, JT and Violet snuggled in his big bed, their hands offering comfort and connection, their lips meeting in affection. They exchanged no words. The union of their bodies was an effortless way to communicate.

Violet didn't return to the problem of how to broach the subject of his father's possible identity theft until almost five in the morning. JT lay on his stomach beside her, hands buried under the pillow, his features softened by sleep. She reclined on her side, head propped in her hand and watched him. Memories of their lovemaking moved through her nerves like a breeze through a weeping willow. Her hormones stirred lazily in response.

Too wide awake to sleep and knowing she'd be tempted to rouse JT if she kept staring at all his naked glory, Violet slipped from the bed and put on a robe. The moratorium regarding her skinny-dipping had been lifted and she padded downstairs. Earlier, their hasty retreat to the bedroom meant that the living room's glass walls had not been closed. Nor had the lights been turned off anywhere. Violet moved through the various rooms and left a trail of darkness in her wake.

The warm night air pressed against her skin as she stripped off the robe and used the stairs to enter the pool. Despite the water's comfortable temperature, she shivered. Swimming had always been both a way to exercise and a method for sorting through whatever problems she was having.

She'd been on both her high school and college swim teams. Maybe she hadn't been the fastest competitor, but driven by a fierce desire to catch her father's attention, she'd worked harder than most. All in vain, of course, because it wasn't as if he'd ever attended a meet. Eventually she'd accepted that their lack of a relationship was her father's loss not hers, and she'd learned a valuable lesson in loyalty. Never would she let anyone down. If she gave her word, she would move heaven and earth to keep it.

Which brought her to the file on Preston Rhodes. Tomorrow she would show JT what it contained. With the stockholder meeting approaching and his father still holding all the cards, if they had the chance to discredit him, they needed to take it. But was JT ready to destroy the last member of his immediate family?

Violet left the pool and grabbed a quick shower in the pool house before returning to the master suite. Dropping the damp towel on the floor, she climbed naked between the sheets. Convinced she'd left and returned without waking JT, she was surprised when his arms snaked around her waist, drawing her firmly against his side.

With his face buried in the crook of her neck, he murmured, "You smell like chlorine."

"Impossible. I showered before coming back here."

"It's barely detectible, but there." He pressed his lips against the pulse in her throat. "I wouldn't have thought you'd have enough energy for a swim. I guess I'll have to do better at wearing you out."

She laughed at the sting of his nip. "I didn't swim. I waded. It isn't always about burning off excess energy. Sometimes it just feels good to hang out and enjoy the scenery."

"Is that what you were doing tonight? Enjoying the scenery?"

"And thinking."

"About what?"

She hesitated, unsure she wanted to disrupt JT's good mood. "About the upcoming stockholders' meeting and the shares we still need."

JT stopped kissing her neck and lay very still. "I don't want you worrying about that. This is my battle to fight, you've done enough."

"This is my fight, too." Although she was certain he was merely trying to protect her, Violet bristled. "Don't shut me out. I can help."

"My father. My problem."

"We're married. Our problem."

"It's a paper marriage."

"Don't do that," she told him, an ache building in her throat. "Don't shut me out."

He heaved a sigh and rolled away from her, coming to rest on his back. She pursued him across the mattress, sitting up so she could peer down at his face. His eyes remained hard, but his hand scooped her hip, thumb moving rhythmically against her waist.

"You never stop pushing, do you?"

She set her left hand on his chest. His grandmother's ring snared the dawning light drifting in through the open window. They both stared at it.

At long last she asked, her voice scarcely rising about a whisper, "Do you want me to?"

They both knew what she wanted to know. Did she take off the ring and walk away from the marriage? Or did she stay and did they both commit to making their relationship grow and strengthen?

"What you're asking from me isn't easy."

"I know." Relief made her dizzy. He hadn't immediately challenged her bluff. "But we're a good team and we need each other."

"You need me?"

"Don't sound so surprised." Being with him she felt a part of something bigger than either of them could ever be alone. "I'm not as unselfish as you believe." She laid her cheek on his chest and snuggled against his side. "You make me feel safe and secure. I know I can count on you."

"You never seem as if you need anyone's help."

"I may be everyone's cheerleader, but once in a while, I appreciate it when someone has my back." She lifted her head and met his gaze. "I like it when you're that someone."

"You know you will always be able to call on me for anything."

She gave him a wistful smile. It wasn't a passionate declaration of love, but it was a heartfelt promise he would never betray. And she accepted at this moment it was everything he was capable of giving.

In close proximity to the kitchen, an extensive covered patio contained a barbeque pit, a seating area with fireplace and flat screen television and a table that seated eight. Unless he was entertaining, JT rarely used the space. Most often he ate a quick meal in the kitchen before heading out to the hotel or the barn. But since Violet had moved in, he'd spent a fair amount of time enjoying all the amenities.

This morning, the table was strewn with bowls of fruit, plates of bacon, eggs and waffles. More food than either of them could eat. But as soon as Violet had handed him the file on his father, he'd lost all appetite.

"This can't be real." He set the file aside and rubbed the bridge of his nose where a headache was starting.

"Maybe," Violet replied, her tone neutral. "Maybe not."

"Have you read the whole thing?"

"Twice."

"It's ridiculous. My father grew up in California. I've heard him speak about his parents and his childhood in Los Angeles. He's not some wannabe thug from Las Vegas."

"That was my exact attitude when Scarlett brought it to my attention. I thought the whole thing was crazy and told her so."

A chill formed in JT's chest. "Who else knows about this?"

Her gaze sharpened as she caught onto his irritation. "Just Harper. She was there when Scarlett gave me the file. You don't need to worry about her. She won't say anything."

"Do you have to share everything about me with your sisters?" His aggrieved tone made her flinch, but his resentment bit too deep for him to apologize. He'd barely gotten comfortable sharing bits of himself with Violet and it made him surly to think that her sisters knew a devastating secret about his father.

"They won't say anything," she said, using her fork to shred the uneaten waffle on her plate.

"I don't know that."

His logical side reminded him that behaving as if he didn't trust her would create problems between them. But he couldn't ignore his emotions as they sliced him with a double-edged sword of alarm and resentment.

"Well, I do."

Hearing the conviction in Violet's tone, JT let the matter drop, recognizing the true source of his disquiet was not Violet or her sisters. He didn't want to believe his father had stolen someone's identity.

Because if his father wasn't just greedy or ambitious, but despicable beyond belief, couldn't that badness have been passed down to his son?

Wasn't JT the reason his mother had died? He'd been acting out, defying her, and she'd died of an overdose. His adult brain could reason that she'd chosen to take the pills, but he was haunted by the question of whether she'd been so upset with him that she'd taken too many. And there was no denying if he'd come home straight after school that day, she might still be alive.

He stared at the information contained in the file about George Barnes and Preston Rhodes and wondered what the reporter from L.A. knew. "When were you planning to call this Charity Rimes person?"

"I thought it was something we should do together. Perhaps even go to Los Angeles and meet with her in person." She shrugged. "Or we could drop it entirely. Like you said, it's ridiculous that your father stole someone's identity in 1970."

Violet was too forthright to be able to hide her confusion or disappointment at his rejection of the information she'd brought him. Nor could JT point to where this surge of loyalty was coming from. What did he think he owed his father? Preston had never done anything with JT's best interests in mind.

"Let me think about it," JT muttered and Violet nodded, the gesture stiff and jerky.

Because if they discovered his father actually was George Barnes, JT would then have to decide if he should send his father to prison or simply use the information to blackmail Preston into stepping down? Neither appealed to JT. He'd much rather defeat his father the old-fashioned way: by being a better businessman.

Violet finished applying her makeup and checked her appearance in the bathroom mirror. She'd done an acceptable job of hiding the dark circles under her eyes caused by her sleepless night, but nothing could be done about the churning in her stomach.

Right after breakfast, JT had headed to the barn where he'd remained for the rest of the day. As difficult as it had been to give him space when her instincts demanded she make him feel better, she'd stayed in the house and hoped he would forgive her for delivering such a difficult message.

Her wait had been in vain. At three she'd discovered that JT had already left for Titanium. He'd gone to work without letting her know he was leaving. That meant she'd have to be patient for a little while longer and hope uncertainty wouldn't eat her alive.

Instead of heading to Fontaine Chic where she knew a hundred decisions awaited her, Violet detoured to Scarlett's hotel and tracked her sister down in the casino. Scarlett would be eager to learn how Violet's conversation with JT had gone and Violet needed a sympathetic ear.

"I was right to fear that JT wouldn't react well to Tiberius's suspicions about Preston," Violet said, as they wound their way past a hundred slot machines to a dessert bar on the second floor. "And I couldn't blame him for being upset with me."

"You did nothing wrong," Scarlett reminded her.

"I feel as if I did. He was upset because you and Harper knew what was in the file and was worried you'd tell someone. He didn't believe me when I told him you wouldn't. I wish he trusted me."

"I'm sure he does. Remember you'd just brought him shocking information about his father. No matter how strained their relationship or how badly he wants his dad to step down as CEO, Preston is still JT's father."

"Is it crazy that I'm afraid the progress we've made in our relationship has been dealt a deadly blow today?"

"Not crazy at all. But I do think you're worrying for nothing." Scarlett looped her arm through Violet's and pulled her before a glass display case loaded with absolutely scrumptious-looking treats. "We'll take one of those chocolate shells filled with white chocolate mousse and a hazelnut gelato-filled cream puff with Kahlua chocolate sauce," Scarlett said to the counter person. Catching Violet staring at her in astonishment, Scarlett grinned. "What? Heartache calls for fancy desserts."

Violet carried the tray of desserts to a table by the window that overlooked the extensive, beautifully landscaped grounds at the back of the hotel. Scarlett arrived seconds later with cups of espresso.

"I don't know why I was so caught off guard by JT's reaction." Violet dug into the white chocolate mousse. "Barely two weeks ago we were little more than casual acquaintances and today I told him his father might be a criminal."

"Do you really think you two have ever been casual?"

Scarlett asked. "You may not have been friends, but there was a strong pull between you. I saw it that night in Baccarat."

"I've been attracted to him since the first time I saw him."

"I'll bet he felt the same way. Wouldn't surprise me if Tiberius warned him off."

"I'm sure the issue never came up."

"So how did you two leave things?"

"JT is deciding if we should contact Charity Rimes."

"What do you think he'll do?"

Violet shook her head. "I think he'll want to do the right thing, but loyalty is really important to him and no matter how complicated their relationship is, JT will feel as if he's betraying his father." She finished the mousse-filled chocolate cup and began on the half of the cream puff Scarlett pushed onto her plate. "You know, I think he was almost as upset that I'm the one delivering this news about his father as he was by the thought that his dad might be a criminal."

"It makes sense," Scarlett said. "He's not a man who wears his heart on his sleeve. Watching you two last night, it was obvious you have pried the oyster out of his shell. He trusts you, but behaviors rooted in childhood trauma are difficult to overcome and the more vulnerable he feels, the more he will overreact if he something scares him." Scarlett's lips curved. "And baby, the way you make him feel terrifies him."

"I don't want him to be afraid." Doing the right thing shouldn't cause this much anxiety and hurt. "I want him to be happy."

"I know, and he'll get there."

But what if he never did? JT hadn't yet learned to make lemonade out of lemons and wasn't ready to rely on her for his wellbeing. The stockholders' meeting was less than a month away. If he refused to let her in, she was convinced he would demand the divorce they'd agreed to in the beginning. And that would be bad. He needed her. She reminded him to laugh and appreciated his romantic soul. And she needed him. He made love to her with a ferocity she'd never known before. In JT's arms, she wasn't a team player. She was a star.

Buoyed by Scarlett's assurances and a great deal of sugar, Violet went about her day with a lighter heart. It wasn't like her to worry about what hadn't happened yet. Obviously JT was rubbing off on her. If only she were having the same effect on him.

At five her cell phone rang. To her delight, JT was calling. She answered, hoping to keep her emotional state from showing up in her voice. "Hello, husband."

"Hello, wife. I'm calling to apologize."

Lightheaded, Violet leaned against a nearby pillar and squeezed her eyes shut. "No need."

"As always, you are patient and understanding, but I simply must insist on making up to you for my bad behavior this morning."

"What did you have in mind?"

"Room service. Your suite. Fifteen minutes?"

"Sounds perfect." After hanging up with him, she called her assistant and rescheduled the next three hours of meetings. Then she raced toward the elevators and jabbed impatiently at the Up button.

Ten minutes later she'd ordered a steak dinner to be served in an hour, dabbed perfume in all the places JT enjoyed exploring and was waiting for him wearing a smile and a nightie that left just enough to the imagination.

Her approach had been perfect because two seconds after he shut her door, he whisked her into his arms and made straight for the bedroom. A half an hour later she sat astride his narrow hips, breathing heavily in the aftermath of a powerful orgasm, feeling him pulse inside her.

"I could get used to this," he said, cupping her face and pulling her down for a long, slow kiss.

"Me on top?" She gave him a cheeky smile.

"You period."

Her heart lurched. It was the closest he'd come to mentioning the future. She drew his lower lip between her teeth and sucked gently. Beneath her, his chest rose and fell unsteadily.

"No reason you can't," she murmured, showing him how much she had to offer.

"I guess it's something we should talk about."

In her head she was screaming, *Please, can we discuss it now?* What came out of her mouth was a restrained, "I'd like that."

When the door chimed announcing their dinner, JT slipped on his pants and went to let in the waiter. Violet took a second to throw on a robe and run a comb through her disheveled hair. By the time she entered the living room, her small table had been set for an intimate dinner for two, complete with candles, crystal and china.

"It smells wonderful," JT commented as he held her chair while she sat down.

Violet lifted the silver dish covers and set them aside. By now she knew JT liked his meat rare and his vegetables steamed seconds beyond crisp. "Sixty-day dry-aged steak straight from Fontaine Chic's award-winning steakhouse," she said. "With sides of potatoes rosti and asparagus with aged Parmesan and browned butter."

"What are these?" JT pointed to three small bowls.

"Red wine sauce, Béarnaise and a truffle sauce that I haven't yet tried."

"Sounds wonderful."

"Only the best for you." And she meant it. "And for dessert—"

"You're all the sweet I need."

With her insides turned to mush, Violet finished, "Berries with cream."

She watched JT put a piece of steak in his mouth and chew reverently. "This is amazing. There's nothing to compare at Titanium."

He was in such a good mood she hated to spoil it with the question that had plagued her all day: what was he going to do about the information Tiberius had dug up on George Barnes?

"I was lucky Chef Baron agreed to open his third restaurant with us," Violet said, squashing her curiosity.

"I'm sure luck had nothing to do with it," JT said. "You can be quite persuasive."

The compliment warmed her faster than a July day on the strip. "When I know what I want, I go after it."

"I'm very aware of that." A lopsided grin tugged at his lips. "In fact, I'm amazed that you haven't asked if I've decided to call Charity Rimes. I imagine you're dying to know."

"I'd be lying if I said it's the furthest thing from my thoughts." She carefully phrased her next words. "But I can't imagine what a difficult choice you have to make."

"If you'd found out Tiberius had done something terrible, what would you do?"

The question was fair, but it left Violet with a terrible conundrum. She'd always had faith in Tiberius. He'd taken her in and loved her like his daughter. Her faith in his honesty had never been shaken.

"I'd like to say that I'd turn him in and never doubt myself for doing so." Violet gave JT's hand a sympathetic squeeze. "But I don't think I'd ever forgive myself for being disloyal."

JT carried her hand to his lips and kissed her palm. "After dinner, let's call Charity Rimes."

"Okay." Delighted that JT trusted her to help, Violet tucked into the meal with gusto. "I'm glad I didn't order a heavy dessert," she said as they dueled over the last berry. "I don't remember the last time I ate so much."

"Everything tasted so good, it was hard to stop."

Leaving the dishes for later, JT tugged Violet toward the couch. Together they sank into its softness. With JT's left arm around her shoulder and his right hand playing absently with the tie of her robe, Violet waited for some sign from JT that he was ready to hear what Charity Rimes had to say.

"Do you think my father belongs in jail?"

"If he stole someone's identity, yes."

JT closed his eyes and for a brief moment sadness blanketed his expression. Violet's chest tightened sympathetically at his pain. She wished she could take it away. She wanted nothing but happiness for him. But she could only offer comfort and support. JT would have to resolve his ambivalence on his own.

"Make the call," he said, his voice hard and determined.

Reluctant to budge from the circle of JT's arm, but knowing she had to act while he was still in a mood to find out what the writer knew, Violet snagged her cell off the coffee table and found Charity's number. She dialed and then held the phone so JT could listen.

"Yes?" A male voice answered.

Violet and JT exchanged a puzzled look. "Hello. I'm looking for Charity Rimes."

"Are you a friend?"

The man's question awakened Violet's anxiety. "Not exactly. My name is Violet Fontaine. She spoke with my father several months ago about a book she was writing. I was hoping to find out what she told him."

"Can't you just ask him?"

She wanted to demand he let her speak to Charity, but

some instinct stopped her. "He died." She left out the part where Tiberius had been murdered.

A long silence followed. At last the man spoke. "I'm sorry about your father, but Charity won't be able to help you right now. She was in an accident. Her car was T-boned by an SUV."

"Is she okay?"

"She has some broken ribs and a head injury that the doctors want to monitor."

JT frowned and stood. Violet's gaze followed his tense form as he paced across the room. She could only imagine his disappointment. Since this morning he'd had to assimilate potentially damning news about his father and decide whether or not to pursue the truth. No matter how damaged their relationship, inside JT was a little boy who'd once looked up to his father.

"Please tell her I hope she'll be okay. Perhaps I can call again at a later date."

"Do you want to leave your number? I can have her call you."

"That would be nice." Violet gave him the numbers for her cell and the direct line to her office phone. When she hung up a gust of air poured from her lungs. "How crazy was that?"

"It appears as if fate has once again beaten me to the punch," JT replied, his voice wearing a frustrated edge.

"We still have over three weeks until the stockholders' meeting and your cousin Phil has promised to throw his vote your way."

"That means we have forty-nine and a half percent. My father wins." He headed to the bedroom and retrieved the rest of his clothes. "I'd better get back to Titanium. There's one last relative I can call. I didn't want to reach out to her, but maybe the favor she will demand in return won't be as bad as I think."

Violet could tell this wasn't the right time to reassure JT that everything would be okay. He was obviously too disappointed in the phone call to Charity Rimes to believe that the future would work itself out for the best.

"I'll see you at home," she called before he shut the door behind him.

After a quick shower, Violet dressed and returned to her office just in time to make the first of her rescheduled meetings. Even though it was hard to concentrate, she gave it her all. JT's problems would work themselves out one way or another. All he needed to do was trust that when the time came, he'd choose the right path.

And what about her? Would he want her beside him? Violet knew she'd better brace herself in case he didn't.

Nine

"He's leaning. You want to lift his inside shoulder," JT called. "Trot him in a tight circle." The young rider did as asked, and JT nodded. "Do you feel him balance himself?"

Her bright smile was answer enough.

JT followed her progress around the area, but his attention wasn't complete. Part of him was thinking about the stockholders' meeting a week away while another portion gnawed on his relationship with Violet and what he wanted for the future.

It was relatively easy to drop his guard with her. Her lack of an agenda, coupled with her unflagging positivity, and ability to distract him from his problems made her company a balm to his troubled soul.

She seemed to understand, though not appreciate, that he possessed secrets he didn't want to share. JT knew it was unfair. She'd given him so much of herself. That he continued to hold back made their relationship uneven. He didn't know how to fix it without risking losing her. But would she eventually get frustrated with him and leave?

In the beginning, they'd agreed to divorce after the

shareholders' meeting. He hadn't yet decided how to ask her to give their marriage a little more time. He'd grown accustomed to having her around.

She'd coaxed him out of his shell. He was happy. But was she? And was it fair of him to take advantage of her generosity and give her little in return?

The question plagued him through the rest of the afternoon. He listed the pros and cons of being married to Violet, pitting logic against emotion and measuring the ratio of risk to reward. In the end, after he'd applied all his business decision-making skills, it all came down to what he needed to be truly happy.

That evening, as he waited for her to show up at Baccarat, he faced the troubling reality of his situation. No matter how many objections he'd unearthed for staying married, the biggest factor in his decision was that he was falling in love with his wife. "Good evening, husband," Violet said, sitting down beside him on the couch. "What has Rick concocted for you tonight?"

JT glanced at the drink in his hand and realized he'd consumed half of it without tasting a drop. "I have no idea."

"Let me." She plucked the glass from his grasp and sipped. "Blissful Ignorance. Plum gin, red wine syrup, egg white, lemon juice, rose water and balsamic. One of my favorites."

He blinked, a little surprised by her memory and vastly turned on by the way she licked her lips and smiled. Everything about her unleashed his desire. No sooner had he figured out one habit that aroused him than she exhibited another. To say she fascinated him would be an understatement.

"A client wants my opinion on a horse that's for sale in Kentucky," he blurt without preliminaries. "And I thought I'd take a side trip to my family's farm outside Louisville."

"I'm sure your family will be happy to see you."

"Come with me."

They could both use a change of scenery and he very much wanted to show her where he'd spent the happiest moments of his childhood.

"I'd like that. When?"

"Tomorrow."

"I'll clear my schedule." Her willingness to drop everything and run off to Kentucky said that she too felt the need to clear her head. "How long has it been since you've visited?"

"About six months. I try to get there a couple times a year." The farm was the only place he'd ever felt completely at home.

"It must be wonderful," Violet said. "I've never seen you look so happy."

"Never?" He lifted her palm to his cheek and gave her a wolfish smile. "Then you'll just have to pay close attention later tonight."

Her eyebrows rose. "I'll make sure I do."

After a night filled with lots of blissful smiles and very little sleep, they boarded the private jet JT's client had sent to take him to Kentucky.

"Nice," Violet murmured, accepting a mimosa from the flight attendant and relaxing into a butter-soft leather chair. "Fontaine owns several corporate jets, but none as nice as this one. Who's your client?"

"She's a member of the royal family of Dubai." JT smiled at Violet's wide-eyed reaction. "A princess who has a passion for horses and show jumping."

"I had no idea you were so well connected."

"We met in Miami many years ago and struck up a friendship. She knew my grandmother's reputation and likes to get my opinion when she's planning on spending six figures on a horse."

"I am impressed." Violet eyed him over the rim of her glass. "And more than a little turned on."

JT chuckled. "Then my work here is done."

The farm where JT was to evaluate the jumper was about an hour away from his family's farm, Briton Green. The plane touched down at the regional airport less than fifteen minutes away and JT's cousin Samantha was waiting to greet them. He dropped the suitcases an instant before she threw her arms around him and hugged him hard. Tall and slender, with long, dark blond hair and an infectious grin, she had always been a whirling dervish of energy.

"It's great to see you." As soon as she stopped choking JT, she turned her attention to Violet. "I'm Samantha."

"Violet. JT talked non-stop about you the whole way here. It's nice to meet you."

"Likewise." Samantha looped her arm through Violet's and drew her toward the waiting SUV.

JT followed the two women at a slower pace. Already he felt as if the weight of the world had fallen from his shoulders and they hadn't even arrived at the farm.

"How are things?" he quizzed as Samantha sped down the highway.

"Wonderful. Dancing Diva had a gorgeous colt. Mom's convinced he's the best foal we've produced in ten years."

"That's saying something." In the last decade, three national champions had been foaled at Briton Green. "I can't wait to see him. What can you tell me about the six-year-old I'm looking at over at Cal Rutledge's place?"

Samantha nodded. "Nice mover. Good legs. Athletic. I think they've had a few issues with his work ethic."

"Meaning?"

"He's lazy."

"Worth what they're asking?"

"I'd offer them thirty-five and see what happens." Samantha had always been a tough bargainer. "Is the princess open to looking at any other horses?"

"Who'd you have in mind?"

"A client of Roger Simmons has a really nice eight-year-old mare. She's done really well in the show ring, but she needs a smart rider. Roger's had trouble finding someone good enough for her."

"Never hurts to look. Any others you can suggest?"

Samantha laughed. "JT, I could keep you busy for a month looking at all the talent we have in the area."

"Unfortunately I don't have a month."

When they arrived at the farm, they were met by his mother's cousin, Phyllis, Samantha's mother. His grandmother and Phyllis's mother, Adele, had been sisters. When JT's grandmother had married and moved to Miami, Adele had stayed and taken over the running of the farm. They'd owned stock in Stone Properties, given to them by JT's grandfather in exchange for startup capital. Tiberius had bought their shares of Stone Properties stock from them months earlier.

JT hugged his aunt and introduced her to Violet. "The farm looks great," he remarked as they entered the large Greek revival house. "Samantha tells me you had a bumper crop of foals this year."

"She's dying to show them off to you." Phyllis led them into the large living room where a maid had just finished setting a pitcher of sweet tea on the sideboard. "Lunch will be served in half an hour. Would you like something to drink?"

Violet accepted a glass of tea and perched on a damask chair. The house had been built in the late 1850s and had all its original furniture. It was a vastly different from Violet's two-year-old, ultramodern hotel and she looked overwhelmed by the history embedded in every inch of the home.

"I see you're wearing my aunt's wedding ring," Phyllis remarked, her expression friendly, but slightly curious. "When JT called to tell us he was coming and bringing his new bride, we were very excited to meet you." She was too well-bred to admit her curiosity, but JT could see her eyes were bright with it.

"I was excited to meet you as well," Violet said. "I know JT spent a lot of time here as a kid."

"Where did you grow up?" Phyllis asked.

"In Las Vegas."

"What do you do there?"

"I manage a hotel and casino on the strip. Fontaine Chic. My grandfather is CEO of Fontaine Resorts and Hotels."

JT could tell Phyllis was surprised at his choice in wife. Before Violet, he'd gone for style over substance. It made it easier to remain unattached. With Violet, he had the best of both worlds. And he was in way over his head.

"That must keep you very busy," Phyllis remarked, glancing in JT's direction. "This one here has a very difficult time tearing himself away for a visit."

"Between Titanium and the ranch, he has way more on his plate than I do." Violet covered his hand with hers. "Most days I'm lucky if see him at all."

"I'm sure he understands that a wife should never be neglected," Phyllis remarked dryly.

No one in the room could have missed what Phyllis referred to. For several seconds there was complete silence. At last Violet spoke.

"It's fortunate that our work schedules are similar," she murmured.

"I'm sure." Phyllis then took pity on her and changed the subject to what was happening with JT's cousins since they'd last spoken.

After lunch, Samantha took them on a tour of the barns. There were three altogether, housing horses owned by JT's family as well as their clients. They began in the mare's barn. Violet lost track of how many horses she'd petted and how many foals she'd seen either peering out from behind their mother or boldly stepping forward to greet the newcomers. She was completely charmed by the time they headed to the training barn.

"Do you ride?" Samantha asked.

In addition to being a breeding farm, Briton Green had an outstanding reputation as a training facility.

"I'm learning." Violet glanced at JT. "He's given me a few lessons."

"She has a good seat for a beginner."

"We should all take a ride later."

JT glanced at his watch. "I don't think we'll have time. I have a four o'clock appointment with Cal to see what he's offering to Husna."

Samantha looked disappointed. "How about you, Violet?"

"I don't mind going alone to my appointment," JT said.

As much as she'd love to see more of the farm by horseback, she'd come on this trip to spend time with JT. "Maybe tomorrow before we leave?"

With that settled, they quickly toured the training barn and then JT and Violet headed out.

"It's easy to see why horses got into your blood," she remarked as they raced along the country highway in the SUV they'd borrowed from Samantha. "There's something so grounding about them."

"They keep you in the moment. A smart rider is one who anticipates that even the most well-mannered horse might react badly to something in his environment."

"I guess focusing on the present is a good thing for all of us to do from time to time." She'd been spending too much time speculating about what would happen in the aftermath of the stockholders' meeting.

"Is that comment meant for me?" he quizzed, without a trace of acidity in his tone.

"Actually, I meant it as a reminder to myself. I've been doing a lot of thinking about the future. Our future," she clarified, searching his expression for some sign that he had picked up on what was troubling her.

"I've given it some thought as well." He stopped speaking, but didn't appear as if he'd said all he intended to so Violet waited him out in silence "The shareholders' meeting is a week away. We agreed to part ways after that."

Violet held her breath, hoping he felt the same way she did. This time JT's pause was longer. She couldn't keep quiet another second.

"I don't want to divorce you."

JT took his gaze off the road and let her see the yearning that filled his eyes. "I feel the same way." He captured her hand and lifted her fingers to his lips. "Having you in my life is the best thing that has happened to me in a long time."

"Me, too." And it made her realize that if she hadn't already been falling in love with JT she never would have suggested they marry in the first place.

"Are you sure you understand what you're getting with me?" JT asked, holding their clasped hands against his chest. "I'm not the easiest man to live with."

"I know." He still had secrets locked up inside him that caused pain and made him retreat from her. She might never know everything about him, but she'd come to terms with that before she'd decided to fight for their marriage. "I also know you don't fully trust me with everything that happened in your past."

"Are you sure you can live with that?"

How could she answer him when she didn't know herself? "I'm going to try."

As if admitting their heart's desire had drained the energy available for conversation, they both lapsed into silence. Violet stared at the green landscape around the car and waited for her rapid heartbeat to return to normal.

JT wanted to stay married. She made him happy. The thought thrilled her. But Violet wasn't a hopeless romantic.

What lay between them still required work and trust in order to grow, but the fact that neither of them appeared ready to throw in the towel gave them a fighting chance.

The conversation in the SUV had cleared the subtle tension between them. To Violet's delight, JT smiled more readily than she'd ever seen and his kisses grew abundantly more plentiful and passionate.

Snuggling with JT beneath the handmade quilt in the guest room, Violet sighed in utter contentment.

"I'd love it if we could come back here and stay longer," she told him. "I've really enjoyed meeting your family and want to get to know them better."

"I think they feel the same way."

"You're lucky to have them." She pondered her own lack of extended family and sighed. "Until Scarlett and Harper came along I didn't have any family but my mom and Tiberius."

"I get why you weren't in contact with the Fontaine family, but what about your mom's relatives?"

"She lost contact with them after coming to Las Vegas. I asked about them a couple times, but it really upset her so I stopped mentioning them." Violet had gotten the feeling that her mother had been running from an unhappy place when she left home.

"I'm sorry you grew up like that."

"It was okay. At the time I didn't know any different. The lack of family didn't really bother me until after college when I was in a friend's wedding." It had been a huge affair with six bridesmaids and groomsmen. The bride had looked radiant walking down the aisle on her father's arm. "I was the only one of the wedding party that wasn't a family member."

"Does it bother you that we got married without your family there?"

Violet didn't have to think about her answer. "A little. Mostly it bothered me that Tiberius wasn't there to give me away."

"When the shareholder meeting is over we should get married again. Properly this time. With friends and family around us."

"You don't have to do this for me." But she was thrilled that he'd suggested it.

"I'm doing it for us. We should make a fresh start." He kissed her on the forehead. "A real marriage deserves a real wedding. Don't you think?"

Violet tilted her head back so she could read JT's expression. His tender smile made her heart hiccup.

"It sounds like a perfect idea."

Ten

JT was in his office reviewing a capital expenditure request for remodeling the exercise room and upgrading the machines when his assistant hailed him on his phone's intercom.

"Mr. Rhodes is on line one."

It was three days until the stockholder meeting and JT remained short of the votes he needed to oust his father as chairman of the board and strip him of his CEO position. Was Preston calling to gloat?

"Hello, Father."

"You didn't really expect to beat me, did you, son?" Preston gave the final word a disparaging twist. "I've taken on much more skilled players than you."

"I've no doubt you have."

"Then you won't be surprised when I tell you that I'm in negotiations to sell Titanium."

"Not surprised at all." JT had known that challenging his father would be a one-shot deal. He either secured the votes to get Preston voted out as chairman or went out on his own. JT wasn't afraid to do the latter. He'd been ready to abandon any hope of saving Stone Properties before Violet had inherited Tiberius's stock.

"I'm sure we can find you a hotel to manage somewhere," Preston said. "I think the general manager of Platinum Macao plans to retire later this year."

JT saw no reason to react to his father's taunt. "I'm certain you have a number of managers who would jump at the chance to take over that hotel. I have several opportunities I can explore."

"Perhaps your wife can find you a job working for Fontaine Resorts and Hotels."

"In fact we've already discussed that," JT lied. Why was his father trying so hard to get him riled up? "Fontaine is negotiating to buy the Lucky Heart. They're planning to demolish it and build a new hotel. They want someone who can oversee the entire process."

More lies. JT had no idea what would become of the Lucky Heart now that Tiberius was dead, but investigating the fabrication would distract his father for a little while.

"You were lucky to marry your heiress when you did."

"Is there anything else you'd like to discuss?" JT glanced at his watch and saw it was almost time to rendezvous with Violet. They'd taken to enjoying late dinners in her suite. "Otherwise I have a meeting I must get to."

"Nothing else. I'll see you in Miami in a few days."

"Looking forward to it." JT hung up without saying goodbye, unsure if it had been worth his effort to try and shake his father's confidence.

Before leaving his office, JT signed off on the exercise room upgrade, then made his way to the first floor and strolled through the casino. As much as he loved the hotel and was proud of all he'd done to turn the property around in the last six years, JT had always known that his time here was limited. As CEO, his father called the shots. JT could stay working for Stone Properties and do what Preston wanted or abandon the company and strike out on his own. Leaving would have been better for him financially and professionally, but he knew his grandfather would want him to stay and loyalty was deeply imbedded in his psyche.

Even at nine o'clock at night the air on the strip hung hot and thick with exhaust and the sweat of many thousands of bodies. JT sucked in a lungful. Leaving Las Vegas had just become inevitable. The investment opportunities he'd been investigating had involved properties in California, Arizona and the Caribbean. He would be traveling a great deal and setting up his corporate office here didn't seem likely.

What did that mean for him and Violet? They had agreed to stay married. Maybe that had been shortsighted of him. Or she'd gotten him so accustomed to thinking positive that he hadn't truly believed he would lose. Tonight they would have to discuss what changes the future would bring.

Violet sent him a text as he entered the suite to say she was running fifteen minutes late and that the dinner she'd ordered would arrive before she did. JT saw her dining table was littered with copies of Tiberius's files on his family. They'd been going through them the night before, talking strategy. A waste of time. It would take a miracle to topple his father's solid base of supporters.

Was it idiotic of him to ignore the possibility that his father had committed a crime? Preston Rhodes, or George Barnes if he bought into Scarlett's theory, was a ruthless bastard to those who stood in his way. He'd schemed to turn JT's grandfather against his only son. He'd psychologically abused his wife until she'd turned to drugs and alcohol and overdosed. And he'd blackmailed a Stone Properties stockholder to manipulate the annual vote in his favor.

Maybe it was time someone pushed back. And who better than the son he was determined to hurt next.

Not wanting to start their evening by talking about his father, JT gathered the files and carried them into her home office. He set the pile on her desk and was turning to go when a lone file caught his eye.

JT looked closer and went cold as he spied his name in Tiberius's handwriting on the tab.

Violet had a file on him.

If Tiberius had investigated Preston's past, didn't it make sense that he'd have looked at JT as well? And when he'd left his files to Scarlett, of course she would share his file with her sister.

Dread collecting in the pit of his stomach, JT opened the file and stared at the top sheet. It was the police report on his mother's death. They'd ruled it an accidental overdose but right there in black and white was JT's darkest secret.

How long had Violet pretended not to know what he'd done? Had she played him for a fool from the start? Acted as if it was important that he confide in her when she'd already known every agonizing truth of his childhood. Bile rose in JT's throat at her betrayal.

Below the police report was a copy of the psychiatrist's initial assessment when JT had been hospitalized for a severe concussion and broken ribs after trying to jump his bicycle over his father's yellow Ferrari convertible. He'd attempted the risky stunt a month after his mother's death. Based on the timing, the doctor had determined he was depressed and put him on medication. But no pill had been capable of taking away JT's guilt.

A knock sounded on the suite's front door startling JT. For a long black moment he'd been twelve again, hearing the news that his mother was dead. Lightheaded, he backed away from Violet's desk and those horrible childhood memories.

His heart pounded madly as he shook his head to clear it. There was a second knock on the front door. Rousing himself, JT made his way through the living room and let in the waiter. The smell of the food turned his stomach as it passed and he stood in the doorway while the man unloaded the dishes onto the dining room table. Moving on autopilot, JT signed for their dinner and was about to close the door when Violet stepped off the elevator and headed down the hallway towards him.

"It smells wonderful," she said cheerfully, lifting on tiptoe to press her lips to his.

JT stood with his hands at his sides and didn't return her kiss. She pulled back with a frown and surveyed his expression.

"What's happened?" she asked, closing the door.

"You have a file on me."

Guilt flashed across her lovely features and drove a spear into his heart. "Tiberius had a file on all of us."

"All this time you've been lying to me." A heavy note of sadness weighed down his voice.

"That's not true."

"You've known everything all along and pretended you didn't."

"Scarlett gave me the file," Violet explained. "But I've never opened it. If I've done anything wrong it was in not handing over the file to you as soon as I got it."

"You really expect me to believe that you didn't satisfy your curiosity about me by reading what my uncle dug up about my life?"

"If I had, why would I bother to ask you to share your past with me?"

"To make me believe you were the perfect woman for me. It's all in there, you know. The psychologist's report explains that before my mother's death I badly wanted her love and when she chose my father over me I retreated into belligerence and bad behavior. The more I acted out, the less likely it was that anyone would love me. And then you came along, and knowing what I most wanted was what I most feared, you did everything you could to make me trust you."

Violet looked stricken. "You don't know me at all if you believe I would ever manipulate you."

"No? You suggested we get married. You claimed my father threatened to sue us if we didn't act like a real married couple."

Now it was her turn to get angry. "I married you to help you."

"You married me to help yourself."

The part of him she'd touched with her compassion and optimism wanted very much to take her at her word, but he'd been protecting himself against being hurt for so long. It was a compulsion he couldn't resist.

"I spoke with my father tonight and he let me know he's selling Titanium. I'll be leaving Las Vegas to pursue some investment opportunities." He hadn't intended to present the situation so bluntly, but in lieu of what he'd discovered here tonight, he wasn't capable of being sensitive.

"How long will you be gone?"

"This is a permanent move. I'm going to sell the ranch and resettle elsewhere."

Violet recoiled as if he'd struck her. "Just like that without discussing it with me?"

"What would be the point? As per our original agreement as soon as the annual shareholder meeting is over, I'll be filing for divorce."

"Can't we talk about this?"

"There's really no point. Your life, your career is here. I have no reason to stay."

"You really don't get it, do you?" Violet's soft question resonated with compassion.

JT's chest ached to the point where he couldn't draw a full breath. "Get what?" he asked coldly.

"That I love you."

"I'm sorry you said that," JT told her, his voice low and flat.

Violet nodded. "I'm sure you are."

He'd torn out her heart and thrown it at her feet, but Violet wasn't about to let him think he'd won. His mask of indifference might have worked on her once upon a time, but she'd glimpsed his sensitivity. He'd rather be the most hated man on the planet than let people see his vulnerability.

Not that she was immune to what he'd told her. Stung by pain and disillusionment, he was going to isolate himself beyond anyone's ability to reach him. In her heart, she knew that was the last thing he wanted. If she'd shown him anything, it was that being alone only made him miserable.

"I don't think I'll stay for dinner." He stepped around her and put his hand on the doorknob.

"Before you go." Violet headed to her home office where she found the file that had destroyed any hope of happiness for her or JT. She straightened the pages he'd disrupted while reading and closed the cover. In less than a minute she'd returned with his file and the one on his father. "You should take these with you."

He looked ready to toss more angry words at her, but accepted the files in silence.

"If you need anything, just call," she added as he opened the door and stepped into the hallway.

His back stiffened as if she'd cursed at him. "Goodbye, Violet."

And then he was striding away, his long legs carrying him around the corner and out of sight. Only then did Violet turn into a puddle of shaking limbs and wracking sobs.

She shut the door and slid onto the floor and wrapped her arms around her knees. Drawing a complete breath was impossible so she closed her eyes and let the storm roll over her. By the time she'd calmed enough to pick herself off the floor, half an hour had passed.

She stumbled into the living room and dropped onto the couch. Greeted by silence, she immediately grabbed her phone and texted her sisters.

I messed up. In my suite, could use some sympathetic company.

Harper was the first to respond. Bringing both red and white wine.

Scarlett texted a minute later. Got chocolate.

With a shaky smile Violet rubbed tears from her cheeks. How lucky she was to have two wonderful sisters who dropped everything in order to rush over to make her feel better. Fifteen minutes later, wearing sweats and feeling marginally calmer, Violet opened her door to admit Harper.

"Which one should we start with?" she quizzed holding both bottles out for inspection.

"Definitely the red," Violet replied, knowing Scarlett would vote for that as well. She led the way into the kitchen to find the bottle opener.

"What's with the uneaten dinner?" Harper quizzed.

"JT and I ended things before we had a chance to eat."

"What?" Scarlett demanded from the living room, having come through the door to the hallway Violet had left open. "How is that possible? You two were doing great." Scarlett came into the kitchen, and both her sisters stopped what they were doing.

Harper held up her hand as she took in Scarlett's outfit. "Before we get to that, can you please tell me what you're wearing?"

Scarlett looked surprised at the question. "It's Princess Leia's harem costume from *The Empire Strikes Back*."

"Were you wearing that in the casino?" Violet quizzed, imagining the ruckus her sister must have caused among the male customers.

"Don't be ridiculous. I wore it for Logan."

Harper looked sorry she'd asked.

"I didn't mean to interrupt your evening," Violet said.

"Don't worry about it. Logan understands that a call for help from one of my sisters will never be ignored."

Tears surged in Violet's eyes once more, causing Scarlett to curse and Harper to put her arms around Violet's shoulders.

"You guys are the best," she whispered past the lump in her throat.

Harper poured the wine and the three of them moved to the couch. Snuggled between her sisters, Violet sipped at the excellent red and told them about JT finding his file and accusing her of using its contents to trick him into marriage.

"How does he not realize that if anyone benefited from you two getting together it was him?" Harper demanded hotly.

"He's used to being manipulated," Violet said. "It's made him guarded and secretive."

Harper regarded her in dismay. "You're still defending him?"

"She's in love with him," Scarlett said, patting Violet's knee. "And if anyone is to blame in all this, it's me. I never should have given you his file."

"Not true. I could have given him the file immediately or shredded the thing. He never should have discovered it sitting on my desk."

"But you aren't to blame for the way he reacted," Harper insisted.

"In a strange way, even though I never looked at what was in his file, I feel as if I betrayed him."

Scarlett shook her head. "You're acting far too reasonable. Rant. Cry. Call him terrible names. He deserves it."

That wrung a weak smile from Violet. "You know I'll never do that."

"Any chance this will just blow over?" Harper asked.

Violet exhaled shakily. "Maybe if it had happened weeks ago, but we've grown really close recently. We've talked about the future and agreed to give our marriage a chance."

"That could still happen." Scarlett looked hopeful.

"Preston is selling Titanium. JT has no reason to stay in Las Vegas."

"Bastard," Scarlett muttered. "I think for JT's sake we need to find out the truth about his father."

Before tonight Violet might have protested that it was JT's business not hers, but since he'd called it quits, she no longer had to consider his feelings in the matter. Still, guilt tweaked her. What if he didn't want his father exposed?

"I spoke with Charity Rimes earlier today," Violet admitted. "I was going to talk to JT about it tonight before…"

"What did she have to say?" Scarlett demanded, her expression alive with curiosity. "Why did Tiberius contact her?"

"Remember how she was doing research on a serial killer who was operating in Los Angeles in the sixties? He invaded homes and attacked families. The police never caught him."

"How is that related to Preston?"

"Turns out one of the families killed was named Rhodes. They left behind a ten-year-old son, Preston, who'd been spending the night with a friend."

Harper had been leaning forward, fully engaged. Now

she sank back against the couch cushions with a whoosh of exhaled air. "That's awful."

"Charity was blogging about the families who were killed and Tiberius had been running internet searching on Preston when he stumbled on her."

"So, how does this help us?" Harper persisted.

"After speaking with Tiberius, Charity got curious about Preston and tracked down his high school yearbook."

"And," Scarlet prompted.

"She promised to send me the photo."

Harper prodded. "Did she?"

"After what happened with JT I haven't thought to check."

"Where's your phone?" Harper was on her feet.

"I left it in my home office when I went to get the files for JT."

All three women raced to find Violet's phone. Sure enough, an email from Charity Rimes sat in Violet's inbox. She opened the message and held it so both her sisters could survey the image.

"That's not JT's father," Harper intoned.

Scarlett agreed. "No it's not."

Violet felt a peculiar lightness envelop her. In her hands was a way to save JT. But did he want to be saved? More importantly, would he want to be saved by her?

"We need to go to the police," Harper said.

"Which police?" Scarlett asked. "It won't do us any good to take it to the Las Vegas PD because Preston lives in Miami." She plucked the cell phone from Violet's grip and began typing. "I'm going to send this to Logan. He'll know the best way to handle it."

Twenty minutes later, Scarlett's fiancé sat on the coffee table and scowled at each of the three sisters in turn. When his gaze settled on Scarlett, he growled, "I thought I told you to drop it."

"I did." She gave him a winning smile. "Right after I gave Charity Rimes's phone number to Violet."

Logan sighed and shifted his hard gaze to Violet. "Have you spoken with JT about this?"

"We aren't on speaking terms at the moment."

That seemed to surprise Logan. "He should know what you've discovered."

She shook her head. "I doubt he'll take my call. Would you tell him?"

"You're his wife. It would be better coming from you."

"I'm the woman he married to get access to his family's stock," she corrected him. "And tonight he found out I had a file that Tiberius had put together on him. That I never looked at," she added when Logan's expression grew even grimmer.

"Every one of those files should have been burned," Logan growled, shooting his fiancée an unhappy look.

"What's done is done," Scarlett replied unapologetically. "We need to move forward. Preston Rhodes is an imposter and it's time that caught up with him."

Clad in a towel, JT stood in the enormous walk-in closet off his master suite and stared at the array of feminine fashions that occupied half the space. In addition to Violet's clothes, there were twenty pairs of shoes and assorted purses. Her jewelry was on his bureau, her lingerie in his dresser drawers. The scent of her clung to the sheets. Her cosmetics occupied the bathroom countertops. Traces of her lingered everywhere.

"Damn."

He'd been unable to sleep the night before so he'd sat in his living room, alternately staring out at his empty swimming pool and reading the file Tiberius had put together on Preston. He'd grown queasier with each page he'd turned. A dozen times he'd started to close the file, but then he'd hear Violet's voice and knew he could no long pretend that his father hadn't maliciously sabotaged his competition and blackmailed friends. He'd fled the truth for too long. His father was evil.

Sometime around dawn he'd drifted off. When he woke around six, he'd been having a dream where he chased Violet through a casino, calling her name, but she was always far out of reach. The memory of it left him with a cottony taste in his mouth and an ache in his temples. Interpreting the dream was easy. He'd lost the best woman he'd ever known because he was too closed down to give her the intimacy she deserved.

In the center of the large master suite, his empty king-size bed stood as a reminder of all the things he'd never enjoy again. Violet's body moving beneath him. Her soft moans. The bite of her nails as she climaxed. The brilliance of her smile in the aftermath of their lovemaking. The utter peace he felt with her nestled beside him.

He could burn the sheets, replace the mattress, hell, even toss out all the furniture, but he'd never be free of the mistakes that had led him to shove her away. Worse, he suspected she'd forgive him for being such an ungrateful jerk if he'd just share with her his feelings about what haunted him. But he'd clung to the secret for so long. It was impossible for him to set it free.

For a moment he was almost grateful to his father for selling Titanium. Staying in Las Vegas would have been impossible. Only with a change of scenery could he hope to adapt to life without her. Not that it was going to be easy. He'd given her access to places inside him that no one else had ever seen. Or was that true? Thanks to the file Tiberius had put together on him, didn't she already know all his secrets?

From the nightstand, his cell began to ring. Teeth locked together in irritation, JT left the closet and went to answer it.

"Yes?" he snapped.

There was a momentary pause before a man spoke. "JT? This is Logan Wolfe."

The security expert's connection to the Fontaine family immediately roused JT's suspicion. "What can I do for you, Logan?"

"I was wondering if we could meet. I have something to talk to you about and it shouldn't be done over the phone."

"If this is about Violet, you can forget it. We're done. End of story."

Another short but significant pause followed JT's declaration.

"Actually, this is about your father."

"I don't know what he's up to but he can go to hell. I'm done with him. I'm done with Stone Properties. I'm done with everything." Aware that he was working himself into a rant, JT sucked in a breath to steady his emotions. "Sorry," he muttered more calmly. "It's been a bad twenty-four hours."

"I get it," Logan said, sympathy in his voice. "I was there. And I have to tell you that the way you're feeling right now is not worth taking out on a terrific woman like Violet."

The unsolicited advice was a sucker punch to his gut. "You have no idea what I'm going through."

"Trust me, I do," Logan said, and the words were so heartfelt that JT believed him. "Scarlett and I almost didn't make it because I overreacted to something that happened. I would have been the sorriest son-of-a-bitch on the planet if she hadn't forgiven me for taking it out on her."

JT's anger faded, leaving a sick feeling in his gut. "It's too late. We're over."

"Do you really believe that or is it just fear talking?"

JT had no answer.

After a moment, Logan said, "I know you and your dad

have issues, but he is your father. Do you want to meet with me and hear what I have to say?"

"No. I don't owe him anything."

"Have it your way. Take care, JT." And then he hung up, leaving JT wondering if he was really as done with everything as he thought.

Eleven

The black town car her grandfather had sent to meet her at LaGuardia Airport stopped in front of the building that held Fontaine Resorts and Hotels' corporate headquarters in New York. Without waiting for the driver to open her door, Violet slipped from the back of the vehicle and crossed the sidewalk to the entrance.

Her heart was racing as she passed through security and ascended the elevator to the executive offices on the twentieth floor. She'd been here several times in the last five years, but those had been social visits with her grandfather. Most of her meetings with Fontaine's top executives happened in Las Vegas via video conference.

"You can go right in, Ms. Fontaine," her grandfather's assistant told her. "He's expecting you."

"Hello, Grandfather." By the time Violet crossed the enormous executive office, her grandfather had circled the desk. She walked straight into his arms and hugged him tight.

"My dear Violet." He squeezed back and released her. "You sounded upset on the phone. What's happened?"

"I've done so many things wrong I don't know where to begin."

"Start anywhere. I'll try to keep up." He drew her to the leather couch occupying one side of his office and surveyed her face for a long moment before calling to his assistant. "Jean, can you get Violet a cup of tea?" He settled her on the sofa as if she was a fine piece of porcelain and added, "Something soothing."

Three minutes later Violet cradled a china cup of herbal tea and let the warmth seep into her skin. "Thank you," she murmured. "I'm afraid I'm a bit of a mess these days."

"Why don't you tell me what happened."

"As you know, I married JT Stone so that I could vote the shares of stock Tiberius left to me." Violet could tell her grandfather was making an effort not to offer his opinion on her rash action. "It started out as a business deal."

"And then you fell in love."

Violet nodded. "He's very guarded and has a hard time trusting because of the way his father has always treated him. But I really thought in time I could get through."

"And now you don't believe you can."

"Scarlett gave me some files that she inherited from Tiberius. Apparently there was an entire storage unit filled with thousands of files dating back fifty years. He had one for each of us—" she paused "—even you."

Henry smiled wryly. "I suppose when I entered your life, Tiberius wanted to make sure I wouldn't cause you harm. I rather liked his protective streak. Made me glad that you had someone looking out for you while you were growing up."

Something his own son had failed to do. It went unspoken, but Violet sensed Henry Fontaine was deeply disappointed that Ross had behaved with so little honor.

"When Scarlett started looking through the files, she discovered one on JT and his father. As I've already told you, Tiberius was making a move to take his family's company back from Preston. I think he wanted JT as his partner, but wanted to make sure his nephew wasn't like Preston."

"And JT found out about the file?"

"Scarlett had given it to me. I should have shown it to JT right away but so much happened so fast and I forgot about it. Instead he found out I had it and accused me of using the information to trick him into getting married. Only Scarlett didn't give it to me until after JT and I got married and I never read it." The words tumbled out of her, each sentence coming faster until she ran out of breath.

"I'm sorry things are difficult between you," her grandfather said. "What can I do to help?"

"JT is losing Titanium. Preston is selling it to punish JT for going up against him. I don't think JT cares. He was planning on striking out on his own before I found out Tiberius had left me his stock. But that was before we got married. When Titanium is sold, he's going to leave Las Vegas."

"I'm still not sure how I can help," Henry said gently.

"I'd hoped you'd be able to find out who had shown an interest in Titanium and somehow interfere with the sale. I need some time. The longer JT sticks around, the more chance I have to save my marriage."

"And if he is still determined to go?"

"I belong with him. Wherever that is."

Her grandfather's expression registered surprise at her passionate declaration, but he didn't hesitate before asking, "Are you sure that's what you want to do?"

"Of course." She needed her grandfather to understand why this was important to her. "I love him and whether he believes it or not, he needs me."

"You know what's at stake if you leave Fontaine Chic."

"Any chance to run Fontaine Resorts and Hotels." Violet gave him a sad smile. "In the last year I've stopped see-ing myself in the CEO job. Harper is the one you should choose. She's trained all her life to take over. You won't find anyone more dedicated or driven."

"I must say, I'm surprised."

Violet didn't pretend to wonder what he meant. "I'm not giving up because I feel I'm not capable or because I'm not performing well, but because I recognize the depth of commitment the position requires and I'm reluctant to make those sacrifices."

"I value your honesty, and you're right about the job re-quiring all your time and energy. Since starting the com-pany I've lost my wife and my son and I've had to face that neither relationship was as good as I wished they'd been."

Nodding because her throat was too tight to allow words, Violet smiled at her grandfather. "Thank you for understanding. I was worried that after you gave me such an amazing opportunity, you'd be disappointed in my de-cision."

"You are an intelligent, compassionate woman with a creative, enthusiastic business presence. From the first you've been an asset to the Fontaine team. And I couldn't be more proud to call you my granddaughter. I've had my concerns that your heart might lie in Las Vegas and that you would eventually decide you wished to stay there, in-stead of coming here to assume the role of CEO. But now I see that what you truly love, you commit to, and I want you to understand that whatever happens with JT, you will always be a Fontaine."

His words were a warm embrace and Violet smiled gratefully. "Thank you."

She couldn't help but contrast JT's family experiences with her own. If she'd faced nothing but a string of ridicule and rejection from those who were supposed to love her, would she still wake up each morning feeling optimistic?

Would she be able to create a safe haven that supported her and gave her a place to hide from all the negative words and actions that came at her?

"What are your plans for the rest of the day?" her grandfather asked.

"I thought I would do a little shopping for Scarlett's bridal shower and then head back to the apartment."

"I'll make some calls to see what I can find out about Titanium and meet you there at six. I'd like to take you to dinner. There's a restaurant I'd like your opinion on. I thought perhaps we could discuss the opportunity to open a new restaurant in Fontaine Richesse with the chef."

"Grandfather, I don't know," Violet said with a laugh. "The last chef you found has made Harper's life hell. I'm not sure the food is worth the drama."

"I had no idea she was having trouble."

And maybe Violet shouldn't have spilled the truth. "It's their personalities. Ashton is creative and spontaneous. And even more of a perfectionist than Harper, if you can believe it. He's had input on everything from the font on the menu to the décor and is forever changing things in his obsessive search for better or more spectacular. I'm starting to wonder if they'll ever get the restaurant open."

"Is that why the opening has been postponed two times? She told me there was a problem with the fixtures being delayed."

"Because he changed his mind on what he wanted at the last minute and new things had to be ordered." Violet put a hand on her grandfather's arm. "Please don't tell her I mentioned this. She'd kill me if she knew I'd said anything."

"Ross's neglect made her think she had to prove her worth. Even after his death the need for acceptance drives her hard." Henry's eyes darkened with sadness. "I'll figure out a way to speak with her without letting her know you and I discussed it."

As Violet kissed her grandfather on the cheek, her phone buzzed. Her stomach in knots, she exited his office. She'd been waiting for this call for the last three weeks. What she'd put in motion might not solve her problem with JT, but it was the best way she knew to convince him she had no intention of letting him go without a fight.

JT stepped off the plane he'd chartered to Miami and headed in the direction of the Porsche 911 Cabriolet waiting by the hangar. His cousin Brent leaned his six-foot-two-inch frame against the sports car, arms crossed, looking relaxed and amused at JT's surprise.

"What the hell are you doing here?" JT demanded, enfolding his cousin in a hearty hug, shocked by the strength of his emotion.

Brent looked equally caught off guard, but recovered quickly and gave JT a toothy grin. "Thought you could use a little moral support tomorrow."

"You have no idea."

"Violet couldn't come?"

"She…" What excuse could he give for his wife not being at his side, lending her support, at such a crucial time? He owed Brent the truth. "We're over."

"No way. You two are crazy about each other." Brent's confused dismay added punch to JT's self-doubt. "What happened?"

"It's a long story and better told over drinks." JT circled the car and opened the passenger door. "I've got a suite at the Marriott."

Brent slid his long frame behind the wheel. "You're not staying at Cobalt?" It was the premier Stone Properties hotel in downtown Miami where the stockholders' meeting would take place the next day.

JT grimaced. "That's another story better told with alcohol."

"Sounds like it's going to be a long evening." Brent started the car.

The explanations began when the two men settled into a booth at the hotel's bar. JT figured he'd start with what happened with his father and work his way into the more painful story.

Brent didn't look surprised when JT recounted how Preston had informed him that Titanium was going to be sold. "It's the only property without any significant debt," Brent reflected. "He needs the capital to make the balloon payments coming due."

"Despite how hard I fought to get my father out," JT said, for the first time voicing what had dawned on him several days earlier, "I'm not really sorry to be leaving Stone Properties."

"Really? The last time we talked you were determined to take over. It's your legacy."

JT shook his head. "A tainted one. My father ruined so many lives in order to take over the company. How can I sit in the CEO's chair and not be haunted by what he did to my uncle and countless others?"

"So, you're giving up?"

"I'm moving on." JT offered his cousin a wry smile. "Feel like buying thirty percent of Stone Properties?"

"You own forty-eight percent."

"Eighteen percent of that is Violet's."

"But if you two are divorced, she can no longer vote the shares."

"True." JT's focus sharpened. "Are you telling me you're interested?"

"With restructuring, the company could be made solid once more. I thought you'd want to be the one to do that."

"And now that you know I'm not?"

"I will."

The idea that his cousin wanted to take over Stone Properties gave JT a great deal of satisfaction, but there was still the problem of not having enough shares to remove Preston as chairman of the board. He refrained from bringing it up. The mood at the table had brightened considerably and JT wasn't about to kick sand on the fire.

After several more drinks over which Brent spelled out his plan to fix Stone Properties, JT's cousin grew somber.

"Are you drunk enough to tell me what went wrong between you and Violet?"

"No." JT offered an unhappy smile. "But I'll tell you anyway."

He then explained about Tiberius's files and how Violet had been in possession of one on JT. "She played me."

"How do you figure?"

"Every dirty little secret I have was in that file." All except one. The worst one.

And no one would ever know what happened the day his mother died. How he could have been the one to save her if he hadn't disobeyed her.

"She knew exactly how to make me…" JT stopped. He'd been about to say *make me fall in love with her*. Because that's exactly what had happened. Suddenly he felt ill.

"Make you what?" Brent prompted.

"Make me trust her."

"She seemed pretty trustworthy to me," his cousin said. "Loyal, too."

"She is." JT was aware he wasn't thinking straight. "I mean she seems trustworthy." In fact she had been. Violet hadn't done a single thing to hurt him. Quite the opposite. She'd supported him.

JT dropped his head into his hands. "Oh, hell."

"I'm guessing you just realized you messed up."

So what if she'd had a file on him. So what if she'd memorized the damned thing. The fact that he refused to let her in, to open up his past so she could understand why he retreated the way he did, hadn't left her much choice. Given her open nature, it must have been stressful for her to come up against his defenses day after day. Sure, he'd let her in a little, but that could only have given her hope that he'd share more.

But how could he let her in when what lay hidden was so ugly? He was selfish and filled with bitter anger. His childhood scars made it impossible for anyone to love him, even Violet. So he'd pushed her away.

"I don't feel like drinking anymore," JT said, besieged by the need to retreat and regroup. His nerves were raw and exposed. If he went into the stockholders' meeting like this tomorrow, his father would eat him alive. "I'm heading back to my room."

"Sure." Brent regarded him with concern. "Are you sure you're okay?"

"No, but after some aspirin, a shower and a few hours' sleep, I might be able to get through tomorrow." What happened after that was anyone's guess.

Her grandfather's Gulfstream enabled Violet to arrive in Miami an hour before the shareholders' meeting was set to start. JT wasn't expecting her and she wasn't sure what sort of reception she'd receive. With each mile of road that passed beneath the town car's tires, her anxiety grew until she ran out of time to worry. She'd arrived at Cobalt.

The Stone Properties' flagship hotel was a towering thirty-story structure that overlooked the bright blue waters of Biscayne Bay. Everything about the lush landscaping bordering the circular driveway and the glassed entrance to the lobby was staged to impress. But as Violet exited the town car and headed inside, she noted a dozen tiny flaws in the way the staff conducted themselves and spied the dust lingering in the decorative moldings. At a quick glance everything appeared to be functioning, but Violet's trained eye recognized mismanagement.

Crossing the two-story foyer, Violet made her way to the conference room where the annual meeting was taking place. She picked up her pace when she saw the doors had already closed. If she'd hoped to slip in unobtrusively, she'd underestimated the number of stockholders who would be attending.

There were less than a dozen people scattered throughout the chairs that faced a raised dais with a podium in the middle. Seven pairs of eyes shifted in her direction, but she only cared about a particular pair of hard blue ones.

Simmering with ill-concealed annoyance, JT sat beside his cousin, Brent, half way up on the far side of the room. He didn't look happy to see her, but she hoped that would change when he understood why she was here. She took a seat in the back of the room while Preston ran through the day's agenda. As stockholder meetings went it was fairly routine. They would vote to accept the company's financials as well as several amendments to the bylaws. The agenda had been sent out months ago so no one really needed the review, but clearly Preston Rhodes enjoyed hearing himself speak.

While Preston spoke about the success of the company under his leadership and the direction he was taking Stone Properties in the future, Violet watched JT. He sat like a statue, his expression tight and unreadable. If things had gone differently, she'd be sitting beside him, offering him silent support. Her heart ached at the distance between them.

At long last, the explanation of what they were voting on wound down and they were invited to mark their ballots and bring them up to the ballot box. An external auditor would then count the votes while the shareholders enjoyed a specially prepared lunch. Everyone in the room knew it was all being done to satisfy the bylaws. Preston had control over the majority of the shares. What he wanted was what he would get.

Violet lingered in the back while JT voted, hoping to catch him as he left. A muscle jumped in his jaw as he approached.

"I thought maybe you'd mail in your vote." His gaze searched her face for a second before he leaned forward and kissed her cheek.

The fleeting contact caused a hiccup in Violet's pulse. She wanted so badly to wrap her arms around him and tell him everything would be all right, but he had his guard up.

"I wanted to be here for you."

"That's nice." JT's features softened for a moment, but then his father's laugh reverberated around the rapidly emptying room and JT's expression became like stone once more.

Violet watched her husband with a sinking heart. For a second she thought he might tell her he missed her. It was what she'd flown halfway across the country hoping to hear. What a fool she'd been to think their reunion would be joyful and romantic. "I'd better go vote."

"Of course."

JT's gaze clung to Violet's slender form as she walked away. He told himself to go after her. To beg her to love him. Wasn't her appearance here today proof that she wasn't ready to give up on him? But was it fair to take and take from her and give back nothing in return?

"JT, I was hoping I'd get to see you." A stocky man of average height clapped JT on his shoulder. "Sorry about not being able to swing my vote your way, but your father has been running this company successfully for a lot of years."

Clive Ringwald was the owner of a string of auto parts stores in the Midwest and married to JT's mother's cousin.

An affable man, he was firmly in Preston's camp, believing whatever half-truths or outright lies he was told.

"I understand," he told Clive, but his attention was fixed on Violet.

She'd dropped her ballot in the box and handed some paperwork to the auditor. With a last glance his way, she slipped out the room's second door.

Watching the door close behind her, JT felt his entire world shatter. What the hell was he doing standing here letting Clive prattle on? He loved Violet. He didn't care if she'd read his file and knew every shameful thing about him. She'd known who he was and married him anyway. And here he was, acting like such a stubborn fool when he should be fighting for the woman who'd transformed his life.

Cutting off Clive with a brusque apology, JT moved to intercept Violet in the hallway, but she'd already vanished. Figuring she was heading to the restaurant where lunch was being served, JT raced down the hall to the escalator that led to the ground floor. As he rode it down, he caught a glimpse of her passing through the front doors. He was so intent on catching up to her that he didn't notice Brent waiting for him at the bottom of the escalator until his cousin stepped in front of him.

"The FBI's here." Brent's gaze was troubled. "They're taking your father in. Do you know what the hell is going on?"

JT immediately thought of George Barnes and a reporter in L.A. who might have some information on a man by the name of Preston Rhodes. "I think I do. Where are they?"

Before Brent could answer, his father appeared, flanked by two men in suits. In dazed silence JT watched the trio approach. They'd handcuffed Preston, but there was no question that JT's father was not cowed by the treatment.

"Do you know who I am?" Preston snarled.

The man to the left smirked. "Actually, that's what we'd like to chat with you about."

Preston caught sight of JT and his lips curled in disdain. "I suppose this is your doing."

JT shook his head. "I wish it was." And to his surprise he meant it. "Seems as if all your bad choices have finally caught up with you."

"Tell my assistant to call my lawyer," he snapped before he was out of range.

"You're not really going to do that, are you?" Brent inquired.

"Nope." JT glanced at his cousin. "Can I get a rain check on that drink? I need to catch my wife before she leaves."

"No problem. Give me a call later."

But before taking more than a step, once again, JT was prevented from going after Violet. This time it was the auditor who stopped him.

"Excuse me, but was that Mr. Rhodes I just saw leave?"

"It was."

"But I have the results of the election."

"The stockholders are having lunch in the dining room. Perhaps you'd like to tell them what happened." JT turned to go.

"Before you leave, Mr. Stone, you should know that your father was voted off the board."

JT spun around and stared at the auditor, wondering if he'd heard correctly. Then, JT realized he was grinning like an idiot. "Explain it to him." He indicated Brent. "I have more important things to take care of."

Twelve

Violet was unpacking the last of her personal items from her suite at Fontaine Chic when her husband strode through the bedroom door. She glanced up as his presence filled the master suite and made the very air crackle with energy.

"Hello, husband," she said, her tone matter of fact. "Was your trip successful?"

"You know damned well it was." He tugged his tie loose and shrugged out of his suit jacket. When he looked as if he planned to drop both articles on a nearby chair, Violet moved to take them from him. A gentle tug-of-war ensued between them. "I don't need rescuing," he murmured a second before giving her the win.

"Not anymore," she responded, her voice equally soft.

It was going to be all right, she realized as she hung up his jacket and tie. He hadn't demanded to know what she was doing in his house. He'd simply accepted her presence. Her anxiety quieted.

She came out of the closet and found her husband had stripped off his shirt and was working on his shoes. Her mouth went dry as she took in all his chiseled perfection.

Had it only been a week since they'd last made love? The severe ache in her loins made it seem like a whole lot longer.

His socks landed in a pile next to his shirt as he commented, "The FBI hauled my father in for questioning." JT slipped off his pants. Clad only in his boxer briefs, he carried his discarded clothes into the closet. "Any idea what that was about?"

"You didn't stick around to find out?"

"I was too busy chasing after my wife to care." He reappeared in fully naked glory and stood with his arms crossed, staring at her. "Perhaps you can enlighten me."

It was difficult for her to concentrate with her husband's flawless physique artlessly displayed for her perusal. Did he really intend to stand there like that and have a serious discussion? Her blood heated as she took in the rise and dip of his muscular arms and the flawless definition of his rock hard abs.

"Perhaps you'd like to shower first and then we can talk?" Violet suggested, hoping he'd take the hint that it was a conversation better conducted without distractions.

"Actually, I'd like to hear what you have to say first."

Damn him. Well, two could play at this game. She reached behind her and took ahold of her dress's zipper. His expression didn't change as she unfastened her dress, but when it pooled at her feet, she caught a minute widening of his eyes.

"Charity Rimes finally returned our call a few days ago," she said, unfastening her bra and letting it fall to the ground. She shimmied out of her underwear before continuing. "After Tiberius had contacted her, she'd been intrigued about his theory that George Barnes had taken Preston Rhodes's identity and tracked down George's high school yearbook."

The entire time she was speaking, JT kept his gaze

fixed on hers, and off her naked form. He appeared utterly intent on what she was saying, but there was one part of his anatomy with a mind of its own. To provoke it further, Violet reached up and freed the pins holding her hair in a loose topknot. It cascaded around her shoulders, the strands tickling her sensitive nipples and turning them into hard buds. JT's Adam's apple bobbed.

"When she emailed me a copy of the photo from his graduation, it was obvious that your father is not Preston Rhodes."

"So you called the FBI?"

"No, Scarlett suggested we bring the issue to Logan. He had a buddy in the FBI."

Violet bent down and picked up her dress. As she straightened she thought she heard a strange noise emanating from JT's throat, but when she glanced his way, nothing revealed itself on his face, although his erection had surged higher.

"He called me a few days ago." JT's voice was tight and husky. "I didn't want to hear what he had to say."

"I thought you should know what we intended to do and would take it better from him."

"I was so damned mad at you."

Violet flinched at the intensity of his tone. "I know."

Needing a moment to regroup, she turned and walked to a nearby chair, putting her clothes on it. She felt more than heard JT come up behind her, and when he spoke next, he was mere feet away.

"You had a file on me. I felt betrayed."

"I know," she repeated without turning around. Rehashing their fight would not move them past her poor judgment or his interpretation of what she'd done. "I was a little surprised the FBI moved as fast as they did. I thought for certain they would investigate longer." When his hands gripped her shoulders, there was tension in his fingers.

Alarmed, Violet hurried to explain her motivation. "I know he's your father, but he certainly had no right to be in charge of your family's business."

"I don't need rescuing." JT repeated his earlier declaration and turned her to face him. "Not by you. Not by anyone."

Her temper flared. "That's your whole problem," she said, hitting him with all her pent-up frustration. "You think you're doing fine on your own, that this isolated little world you've built for yourself can keep your heart safe." She put both hands on his chest and shoved hard. He stumbled back a step, his expression reflecting surprise at her fierceness, and she stalked after him. "Well, you're wrong." She wagged her finger a scant inch from his nose and he retreated a few more steps. "You need me." She prowled after him, all her heartache and worry rising to a boiling point. "Admit it. Damn you. Admit it."

JT stopped retreating and stood staring down at her face. His fingertips brushed her cheek and came away damp. Violet didn't even realize she was crying.

"I don't just need you," JT said, bending down and lifting her onto his shoulder in a fireman's carry.

He dumped her on the bed and pounced on her. Violet gasped; his rough handling had disrupted the efficient working of her lungs. Or maybe she couldn't breathe because of the way he was staring at her: as if she was the most amazing sight he'd ever seen.

"I don't just need you," JT repeated, his tone tender. "I can't live without you. And I swear I'll do whatever it takes to make sure I never have to."

And then he was kissing her passionately, reverently, without holding back any emotion. Violet's joy knew no bounds as she realized that he'd stopped running from her. He might not have let go of the pain that kept him isolated, but he was ready to let her help him heal.

Her tongue met every greedy thrust of his, devouring just as fervently as she was devoured. With her fingers fisted in his hair, she threw back her head and moaned as his teeth nipped at her throat and he investigated the level of her arousal. Her hips bucked as he slid one finger inside her, then two.

Heat built beneath her skin as his mouth latched onto one of her nipples. The firm tug sent a spear of longing straight down to her core. She twisted beneath him, pinned to the mattress by his weight, but managing to communicate her hunger.

"Now," she commanded breathlessly. "Don't make me wait any longer."

He used his knees to spread her thighs wide, opening her for his possession. "It's been hell for me as well."

And then he was thrusting inside her in one long, measured surge that nearly made her black out, such was her pleasure.

"Yes," she murmured, smiling as his lips claimed hers once more.

He retreated at a deliberate pace, letting her savor the friction of their joining before plunging fully inside her once more. Their union couldn't be measured by the pleasure he brought her body, but by the way her heart swelled to almost bursting.

"I love you," she told him, meeting his gaze as they danced together, hips moving in ancient rhythm.

JT laced his fingers with hers and set their hands on the pillow beside her head. Without breaking his steady stroke into her body, he kissed her gently on the lips before murmuring, "You're my everything."

His confession caused her body to spasm. Her orgasm rolled over her in slow waves of ever- increasing pleasure that slowly faded. When she opened her eyes, she found JT watching her. Her lips curved at the wonder in his expression. He began to move against her powerfully, chasing his own finish. In seconds his body shuddered as his climax claimed him. He let her watch every emotion play across his face.

Breathing harshly, JT collapsed on his stomach beside her on the bed. He peered at her from beneath his long lashes, a wryness in his expression making him look younger than his thirty years. Or, Violet corrected, he looked exactly the age he was and she'd grown accustomed to how stress and unhappiness had made him seem older.

She rolled over on her side and cupped her hands beneath her cheek. "I'm here to stay."

"I assumed that when I saw all the packing boxes in the hall."

"And by here I mean wherever you are." Her lips firmed. "I fully intend to fight dirty if that's what it takes to save our marriage."

"There's nothing to save." He lifted one hand to forestall her heated rebuttal. "Let me finish. I simply mean that I was wrong to push you away and that I'm fully committed to spending the rest of my life with you."

Violet let him see her delight. "Good. I think you made a wise choice."

"So do I." JT rolled onto his side until their noses were an inch apart. His heart rate had returned to its regular resting pace, but every third beat or so it skipped a little as he realized just how happy he was.

"Feel like telling me how the shareholder vote worked out?"

Why did he get the sense that she already knew?

"Strangely enough, it came out in our favor."

"Really?" She did a lousy job of sounding surprised. "How is that possible?"

"From what Brent was able to gather after I left, Casey didn't vote his shares."

"That's odd. Any idea what happened?"

JT decided Violet's poker face was improving, but he knew her well enough to pick up on the trace of amusement in her eyes.

"I don't know if you remember but he was in the midst of a nasty divorce."

"I seem to recall something about that."

Now JT knew she'd been up to something because she'd been the one to point that out to him in the first place. "He let his wife have his four percent of Stone Properties stock in the settlement."

"You don't say." Violet looked suitably fascinated. "But if his ex-wife had the shares, she wouldn't be able to vote them because she was no longer family."

"True." JT let the rest of his explanation hang in the air, but Violet didn't press him to continue. And why would she? JT suspected she already knew how it ended. "Without Casey's four percent, my father and I controlled an equal number of shares."

"So how did we win?"

"That's an excellent question. Perhaps you'd like to explain to me."

"Me?" She sounded innocent, but a smug smile tugged at her lips. "Why would you think I had anything to do with it?"

"Because I've met the ex-Mrs. Casey Stone and she's greedy and beautiful, but not particularly bright. I don't understand why she wanted the shares at all."

"Well…" Violet drew out the word, reveling in the telling of her tale. "It seems that a year ago Casey had bought a big, beautiful love nest for his new amore and hadn't declared it as part of the divorce settlement. So, I let Brittany know and suggested that she might want to ask for the Stone Property shares and let Casey have the house."

"And he went for that? The shares had to be worth more or that was one hell of a house."

"He was in a hurry to remarry, and he stood to lose big because he hadn't disclosed the house." Violet shook her head. "Brittany was thrilled to sell me the stock. After all, I'd done her a good turn. And in the end, I think she received more than Casey intended for her to have."

"You own the four percent?"

"I do."

"This wasn't something you managed overnight, was it?" JT didn't wait for her to answer. "After I told you it wasn't worth pursuing, you went behind my back, didn't you?"

"You refused to let me help."

"And now I see I was wrong." As much as he hated admitting that, Violet's delight took the sting away.

"Good. Maybe now you'll start listening to my advice."

"Yes, oh wise one."

JT put his arms around her and softly nuzzled the side of her neck. She smelled like fresh-cut grass and summer sunshine, both favorite scents from his time on the farm in Kentucky. Lulled by the steady beat of her heart against his, JT felt the door to his most guarded secrets crack open.

"I don't know how to thank you," he told her, strangely at peace now that he was on the verge of telling her about the worst moment of his life.

"You don't have to thank me. I'm your wife. I'll always have your back."

"Then you should know what you're letting yourself in for."

"You don't think I do?" Violet's breath fell against his skin in a soothing cadence. "I didn't read your file, but I know that you're more troubled than the average person by mistakes you've made and that you carry childhood hurts that may never heal."

"I'm more troubled because the mistakes I've made aren't forgivable."

"That's impossible for me to believe."

He never stopped being astonished by her faith in him, but she needed to know everything. "The day my mother died…"

"JT." She cupped his cheek, offering comfort, and drew her thumb across his lips, silencing him. "You don't have to tell me."

"But I do. You were right about my needing to let go of the past. I can't do that if I continue to let fear hold me captive. I need you to know what happened with my mother." He pressed a kiss into her palm and closed his eyes. "I was the reason she died."

Violet's body jerked in reaction to his words, but instead of pushing him away, she moved even closer as if she wanted to slide under his skin and share the burden with him.

"That morning, she confronted me about using her credit card without asking and charging five hundred dollars' worth of video games. She didn't care that I'd bought the games, but the fact that I'd lied about it when she caught me made her angrier than I'd ever seen her. She'd found the games in my room and while I watched she threw them away. Then she told me I wasn't allowed to go on a weekend trip with my friends to Universal Studios Orlando. We were supposed to leave from school that afternoon. I don't remember ever being that mad."

JT sucked in an unsteady breath as memories of that morning washed over him. They were crystal-clear and razor-sharp as if the fight had happened yesterday, not eighteen years earlier.

"I can see why she grounded you and I understand why you were upset, but I don't see how it's your fault that she died. She overdosed. You had nothing to do with that."

"I upset her. I told her I hated her and that I understood why Dad couldn't stand to be around her."

JT shook his head, but there was no denying what he'd done. For a moment he couldn't breathe. His throat had tightened past the point of pain. He'd never told anyone the role he'd played in his mother's death. He needed to claw through years of self-loathing to let it out. It felt as if his insides were shredded.

When he continued, his voice was thick with anguish. "Then I grabbed my backpack and acted like I was leaving for school, but I snuck back to my room and packed what I would need for the weekend."

"You went anyway?"

"I figured she'd be so out of it by the middle of the afternoon, she'd never realize that I wasn't home until I was long gone. By five that evening she was dead. No one found her until the next morning when the housekeeper showed up."

"You were twelve," Violet said. "Your mother was a troubled woman who retreated into drugs and alcohol to cope with an abusive husband. How can you think you were to blame?"

"I overheard someone talking at her funeral. I realized that if I'd come home after school like I was supposed to, I could have found her still alive and called 911."

A tear slid down his cheek. Before he could lift his hand to sweep the dampness away, Violet cupped his face in a fierce grip.

"JT, your mother was an addict. She could have overdosed at any time. You were not responsible for her illness."

He heaved an unsteady breath. Part of him recognized that she was right, and he sensed her love and support would help him forgive himself.

"I love you," he told her, speaking the words out loud for the first time.

Tears filled her eyes, but her smile was brighter than the sun. She wrapped her arms around his neck and hugged him hard. "I can't tell you how much I've needed to hear you say that."

"It's taken me a long time to understand what I was feeling," he murmured into her hair. "Before you came along, the emotions I was most familiar with were dark ones."

"All that is behind us now," she said crisply, her optimism revving up. She leaned back and regarded him, her eyes determined. "Starting today, we have an abundance of new adventures awaiting us. Starting with house-hunting in Miami. I spoke with Grandfather about acquiring some property downtown and building a Fontaine property."

"About that." JT hadn't expected her to be so enthusiastic about leaving Las Vegas for Miami and was worried that his news might not be what she wanted to hear. "We're not going to Miami."

"Why not? Now that your father has lost his chairmanship and is probably going to face jail time, the company is yours."

"Here's the thing. The night before the annual meeting, Brent and I had a long chat about the future of Stone Properties. We came to the conclusion that it would be better served with him at the helm."

"But...but..." she sputtered, "it was your grandfather who started Stone Properties."

"And with Brent running things it goes back into family hands."

She cocked her head and regarded him. "What are you planning to do?"

"What I told you I was going to do before the shareholders' meeting. Get out."

"I see." But it was obvious she didn't. "So, where are we going?"

He soothed her worries with a smile and the stroke of his palm along her arm. "Nowhere. Neither one of us is leaving Las Vegas. In fact, I've decided to sell my shares of Stone Properties and buy Titanium."

Her smile was blinding. "I think that's a wonderful idea. But are you sure you want to settle for one property when you could be in charge of a dozen?"

"With Brent at the helm, Stone Properties will be in good hands. And I'm not really a sit-in-an-office-and-do-nothing-but-read-reports-and-make-policies kind of guy. I like the pulse of Las Vegas and have decided whatever else I do, here's where my headquarters will be."

Violet frowned. "That's all well and good, but what happens if I win Grandfather's contest and take over Fontaine Resorts and Hotels? I'll have to move to New York City. What becomes of us then?"

JT had never considered that possibility. It wasn't that he lacked faith in Violet's abilities to do the job or her grandfather's shortsightedness in not recognizing her talents, but she'd always seemed as much a part of Las Vegas as the strip itself.

"I guess I'll have to rethink my plans."

Her eyes softened. "You'd do that for me?"

"Did you not hear me when I said I can't live without you?"

She snuggled closer and kissed his lips. "Then you'll be happy to know that we'll be living together in Las Vegas. I spoke with Grandfather and bowed out of the CEO race."

"Why did you do that?"

"Because I made you my priority. Whatever you want to do, wherever you want to go, I intend to be by your side supporting you."

"I feel the same way."

She laughed. "Then I guess we're pretty lucky that we both love Las Vegas so much because this is where we're going to raise our children and grow old together."

Her vision of their future was so much better than any he'd ever dreamed of. Gone were the shadows that had kept him from believing he deserved to be happy. Violet's love had banished every one.

JT's arms tightened around her. "I can't imagine anything better than that."

* * * * *

If you liked Violet's story, don't miss her sister's tale:
AT ODDS WITH THE HEIRESS
Available now from Cat Schield
and Harlequin Desire!

COMING NEXT MONTH FROM

HARLEQUIN®

Desire

Available June 3, 2014

#2305 MY FAIR BILLIONAIRE
by Elizabeth Bevarly
To land his biggest deal, self-made billionaire Peyton needs to convince high society he's one of them. With help from Ava, his old nemesis, Peyton transforms himself, but is it him or his makeover that captures Ava's heart?

#2306 EXPECTING THE CEO'S CHILD
Dynasties: The Lassiters • by Yvonne Lindsay
When celeb CEO Dylan Lassiter learns Jenny's pregnant after their one night together, he proposes. To keep her past a secret, media-shy Jenny refuses him. But Dylan will only accept "I do" for an answer!

#2307 BABY FOR KEEPS
Billionaires and Babies • by Janice Maynard
Wealthy Dylan Kavanagh loves being a hero, so when single mom Mia needs help, Dylan offers her a room—at his place. But close proximity soon has Dylan thinking about making this little family his—for keeps.

#2308 THE TEXAN'S FORBIDDEN FIANCÉE
Lone Star Legends • by Sara Orwig
Jake and Madison once loved each other, until their families' feud tore them apart. Now, years later, the sexy rancher is back, wanting Madison's oil-rich ranch—and the possibility of a second chance!

#2309 A BRIDE FOR THE BLACK SHEEP BROTHER
At Cain's Command • by Emily McKay
To succeed in business, Cooper Larson strikes a deal with his former sister-in-law, the perfect society woman. When sparks fly, they're both shocked, but Cooper will have to risk everything to prove it's her and not her status he covets.

#2310 A SINFUL SEDUCTION
by Elizabeth Lane
When wealthy philanthropist Cal Jeffords tracks down the woman he believes embezzled millions from his foundation, he only wants the missing money. Then he wants her. But can he trust her innocence?

YOU CAN FIND MORE INFORMATION ON UPCOMING HARLEQUIN® TITLES, FREE EXCERPTS AND MORE AT WWW.HARLEQUIN.COM.

HDCNM0514

REQUEST YOUR FREE BOOKS!

2 FREE NOVELS PLUS 2 FREE GIFTS!

HARLEQUIN®

Desire

ALWAYS POWERFUL, PASSIONATE AND PROVOCATIVE

HD13R

SPECIAL EXCERPT FROM

 HARLEQUIN

Desire

Read on for a sneak peek at **USA TODAY** *bestselling author Yvonne Lindsay's EXPECTING THE CEO'S CHILD, the third novel in Harlequin Desire's* **DYNASTIES: THE LASSITERS** *series.*

CEO restaurateur Dylan Lassiter is in for a big surprise from a fling he can't forget…

The sound of the door buzzer alerted Jenna to a customer out front. She pasted a smile on her face and walked out into the showroom only to feel the smile freeze in place as she recognized Dylan Lassiter, in all his decadent glory, standing with his back to her, his attention apparently captured by the ready-made bouquets she kept in the refrigerated unit along one wall.

Her reaction was instantaneous—heat, desire and shock each flooded her in turn. The last time she'd seen him had been in the coat closet where they'd impulsively sought refuge, releasing the sexual energy that had ignited so dangerously and suddenly between them.

"Can I help you?" she asked, feigning a lack of recognition right up until the moment he turned around and impaled her with those cerulean-blue eyes of his.

Her mouth dried. It was a crime against nature that any man could look so beautiful and so masculine all at the same time.

A hank of softly curling hair fell across his high forehead, making her hand itch to smooth it back, to then trace the stubbled line of his jaw.

She'd spent the past two and a half months in a state of disbelief at her actions. It had literally been a one-night *stand*, she reminded herself cynically. The coat closet hadn't allowed for anything else. Her body still remembered every second of how he'd made her feel—and reacted in kind again.

"Jenna," Dylan acknowledged with a slow nod of his head, his gaze not moving from her face for a second.

"Dylan," she said, feigning surprise. "What brings you back to Cheyenne?"

The instant she said the words she silently groaned. Of course he was here for the opening of his new restaurant. The local chamber of commerce—heck, the whole town—was abuzz with the news. She'd tried to ignore anything Lassiter-related for weeks now, but there was no ignoring the man in front of her.

The father of her unborn child.

Don't miss EXPECTING THE CEO'S CHILD
by Yvonne Lindsay, available June 2014.

Wherever Harlequin® Desire
books and ebooks are sold.

HARLEQUIN®

Desire

ALWAYS POWERFUL, PASSIONATE AND PROVOCATIVE.

BABY FOR KEEPS
Billionaires and Babies
by **Janice Maynard**

"I have a proposition for you."

Wealthy Dylan Kavanagh loves being a hero, so when single mom Mia needs help, Dylan offers her a room—at his place. But close proximity soon has Dylan thinking about making this little family his—for keeps.

Look for
BABY FOR KEEPS
in June 2014, from Harlequin® Desire!
Wherever books and ebooks are sold.

Don't miss other scandalous titles from the
Billionaires and Babies miniseries,
available now wherever books and ebooks are sold.

Billionaires and Babies: Powerful men…wrapped around their babies' little fingers

HARLEQUIN®
Desire

ALWAYS POWERFUL, PASSIONATE AND PROVOCATIVE.

MY FAIR BILLIONAIRE
by Elizabeth Bevarly

**She was still classy. She was still beautiful.
She was still out of his league.**

In high school, Ava may have been Payton's personal
mean girl by day, but a different kind of spark flew at
night. Now the tables have turned and Payton's about
to make his first billion while Ava's living a bit more
humbly. He needs her to teach him how to pass in high
society, if they can manage to put old rivalries to bed. It's
clear to both that chemistry wasn't just for second period,
but will Payton still want her when he learns about the
scandal that sent Ava from riches to rags?

Look for
MY FAIR BILLIONAIRE
by Elizabeth Bevarly, in June 2014 from,
Harlequin® Desire.

HD73318